THE RIDGERUNNER

THE RIDGERUNNER

RAY HOGAN

THORNDIKE
CHIVERS

FIC
HOG

This Large Print edition is published by Thorndike Press, Waterville, Maine, USA and by BBC Audiobooks Ltd, Bath, England.
Thorndike Press, a part of Gale, Cengage Learning.

The text of this Large Print edition is unabridged.
Other aspects of the book may vary from the original edition.
Set in 16 pt. Plantin.
Printed on permanent paper.

LIBRARY OF CONGRESS CATALOGING-IN-PUBLICATION DATA

Hogan, Ray, 1908–
  The ridgerunner / by Ray Hogan.
    p. cm. — (Thorndike Press large print western)
  ISBN-13: 978-1-4104-1598-1 (alk. paper)
  ISBN-10: 1-4104-1598-8 (alk. paper)
  1. Large type books. I. Title.
PS3558.O3473R55 2009
  813'.54—dc22   2009007009

BRITISH LIBRARY CATALOGUING-IN-PUBLICATION DATA AVAILABLE

Published in 2009 in the U.S. by arrangement with Golden West Literary Agency.
Published in 2009 in the U.K. by arrangement with Golden West Literary Agency.

U.K. Hardcover: 978 1 408 44240 1 (Chivers Large Print)
U.K. Softcover: 978 1 408 44241 8 (Camden Large Print)

Printed in the United States of America
1 2 3 4 5 6 7 13 12 11 10 09

A12005286325

THE RIDGERUNNER

1

A man changes a great deal in five years — a town very little.

Such a thought came to John Locke that September morning as he sat on his blaze-faced bay horse and looked down upon the settlement of Three Forks. The same dusty street; the same collection of weatherworn, frame buildings and houses and corrals all thoroughly savaged by the winds of winter, the blazing suns of summer.

From the crown of the low hill where he had paused he could see no difference. He had grown up in Three Forks, or rather nearby it and had always considered it home although he had been born in Ohio. His parents had trekked westward when he was scarcely five years of age. There had been a massacre, the upshot of which was that the orphaned Locke boy had been taken over by Tom Whitcomb and his wife to raise. He had grown up on the Whitcomb ranch, some miles north of the town, along with their two sons, Starr and Bert.

Blood brothers could have been no closer than those three and Bert and John Locke, because they were almost of identical age, were inseparable during their growing up time. Starr, five years their senior, looked after them with paternal care. The Whitcombs had died, victims of a runaway horse accident, when John and Bert were fifteen and the ownership of the ranch passed on to Starr. It was a share-and-share-alike affair between the three of them. It worked well. The spread grew, prospered. And then Sally Dean and her parents moved into Three Forks.

Fred Dean, coming west with his family from Missouri, bought out Hoiston's General Store. He remodeled the interior, shipped in fresh stock, organized a new and different plan of purchase and payment and very quickly became one of the most important men in that section of the Territory.

But his effect upon the country was no greater than that of his daughter upon John Locke and Bert Whitcomb. Both fell in love with her and she, equally with them, it appeared. But when the time for truth presented itself, she had preferred Bert. John Locke, when the day for the wedding was announced, wished them both luck and rode out of their lives. He knew he could not remain on the ranch; he would not jeopardize the happiness of two people he loved very much with his presence.

Now, after five years, he was back. But only for hours. He was passing through enroute to a fine job as foreman of a large ranch in Wyoming. It meant everything to him, this assuming the ramrod's position on a spread such as the Walking W; it not only paid well and gave him the recognition he had fought so long to obtain, but was also the realization of a pressing, long-standing ambition.

He had trained hard for just such an opportunity; he had learned to handle men, cattle and a gun with equal facility, his skill in the latter accomplishment spreading with unwarranted speed along the routes he happened to travel. But that part to him meant nothing. It was only a phase, a piece of the whole; the job with the Walking W was the culmination of the dream. And while his happiness and pride was unbounded, it was yet incomplete; there was no other to share it with him.

And likely there never would be.

In his thoughts and memory there was only one woman — Sally. Through the years the remembrance of her had never left him although he had tried to forget. He had told himself she was forever beyond his reach, that she was married, the wife of his best friend, a man almost his blood brother, in fact. She could never be his. But he had learned that memory is a stubborn thing.

He sighed, turned his glance then to the long, squat building near the center of town. DEAN'S GENERAL STORE, the sign upon it read. Her father was still there, still doing business. He would stop as he rode through and pay his respects to Fred Dean. He had always liked the Missourian. Then he would move on to the Whitcomb place. He would stay only a few hours. He was already several days late in getting to Wyoming but a few minutes more wouldn't matter.

It would be good to see Starr again. And Bert and Sally. He had thought about her a great deal those last few days when he had decided to drop by Three Forks on his way north. He wasn't certain if seeing Sally again was the wisest thing. It could stir the old fires to an even brighter glow. And it could quench them once and for all time to come, he also knew. In the end he had decided he would do it. It could be the end of the terrible, long-reaching loneliness that sometimes engulfed him.

He urged the bay into forward motion, rode down off the low hill and into Three Forks' single main street. Again he halted, a tall man in the saddle, broad-shouldered, with the sunlight pointing up the blondness of his hair and turning the lightness of his eyes to pale amber. There was an easy slackness about John Locke, a quiet sort of confidence that seeped from the man and laid an aura of capability and suppressed violence about him. Yet there was an unmistakable friendliness that showed through the crinkles at the corners of his long mouth.

It struck him that there was an unusual amount of activity in the town for that hour of the day. Several people walked along through the ankle-deep dust, others stood before the various business firms, deep in conversation. A half a dozen horses were at the rail in front of Frank Chance's Saloon and there was one, he noted, wearing full harness but attached to no wagon, at the jail.

He gave this a moment's consideration and then clucked the bay into movement once more and rode slowly down the middle of the street. A few persons turned to stare briefly at him, most with no sign of recognition, a few others with faint, wondering frowns. He angled the bay for Chance's

11

place and pulled up beside the other horses. He swung down, looped the reins over the bar and halted, letting the half a dozen old men on the saloon's gallery, have their hard, curious look at him. That done, he crossed the wide porch and pushed through the swinging doors.

There were a dozen or so customers, all at the bar. Locke glanced at them, recognized none and hooked his elbows on the edge of the polished counter.

"Beer," he said to the balding, white aproned bartender.

The man drew a mug of the foaming brew, slid it to him. Locke laid a coin down, pinned it with his thumb to hold the barkeep's attention.

"Frank around?"

The bartender shrugged. "Somewheres."

"Any particular place I might look?"

"Try the marshal's office. Something going on around here this morning. Lot of excitement."

Locke released the coin. "What kind of excitement?"

"Ain't heard it all yet. Holdup or something. Couple of men got shot up." The bartender paused, looked beyond Locke's shoulder. "Reckon we'll get the straight of it now. Here comes Luke Ford. He's the marshal's deputy. He'll know what it's all about."

Locke half turned. Luke Ford. A familiar name. He had been the deputy marshal for many years. A bitter, unpleasant man, he had resented very much the town council's selection of Hazen Carey as marshal, feeling that he, as a deputy at the time the preceding lawman resigned, was entitled to the job. He had made an issue of the matter but the council had taken on Carey regardless, believing the outsider's vast experience and reputation by far outweighed Ford's seniority claim. That had taken place a year or so before Locke had ridden on and he would never forget the rancor and bitterness he had seen in Luke Ford.

Luke had changed little. Heavier, his face more deeply lined, his mouth grimmer, he looked much the same as he did that day when he stood before the jail and said "good riddance" when told John Locke was leaving the country. There had never been any friendship between Ford and himself, just why, John Locke was never able to find out. He thought once it was some sort of jealousy but he was never able to find out. He watched the deputy walk up slowly, felt the man's hard, thrusting gaze upon him. Ford had not changed in his feelings, he could

13

see that.

"Hello, Luke," he greeted the deputy and extended his hand.

Ford halted an arm's length away, making no effort to accept the salutation. He stared at Locke through narrowed eyes.

"Five years make that much difference in me? Name is Locke. Used to live with the Whitcombs."

"I know who you are," Ford replied in a low voice. "Turn around, slow. Put your hands flat on the bar."

Locke frowned. He made no move to comply with the order. Color gradually faded from his face and the skin around his mouth began to show whitely. "What's this all about?" he asked in a level voice.

The deputy said, "You'll find out. Now, put your hands on the bar, like I said."

Locke studied the man's taut features. He was half crouched. His right hand rested upon the butt of the pistol at his hip. He was ready to draw and fire at the slightest provocation. Anger began to stir through him and then he brushed it aside. There was some mistake. There was no call for them to be coming after him. He shook his head.

"You're making a mistake, Luke. You got your ropes crossed somewhere."

"Maybe," Ford murmured. "We'll let the

14

marshal decide that."

"The marshal?"

"He sent me to bring you in when he saw you ridin' down the street. That's all I know about it." The deputy paused, looked sharply at Locke. "You comin' along or do we have trouble?"

Locke considered for a moment, shrugged. Trouble and delay was something he could not afford. He was already overdue at the Walking W. Better to straighten this out with the marshal and get it over with. He turned, placed his hands, palms down, on the counter. Ford reached out, plucked his gun from its holster, thrust it into his own belt.

The deputy said, "Let's go," and motioned for the door.

Locke came back around. "Man's got a right to know what he's being arrested for —"

"Ain't nobody arrestin' you yet," Ford cut in. "Marshal just wants to talk to you. Figures it's kind of odd, you turnin' up here this mornin'."

"Odd? What's odd about a man riding through a town? Happens every day. Didn't plan on being around more than a couple or three hours, just long enough to speak to a few old friends."

Ford wagged his head. "Don't be askin'

15

me any why's and what's. I don't know what he's got on his mind. All I know is that he told me to bring you in."

"Must be some reason."

Ford gestured toward the swinging doors again. "Well this much I know. There was a holdup and killin' this mornin'. Four men stopped the Dangerfield stage. Got a wad of money and shot up the driver and guard."

"What's that got to do with me?"

"Before the driver died he said he recognized two of the outlaws. Said they was Starr and Bert Whitcomb. Now, you bein' just like a brother of their's and showin' up here right when you did, sure does look a mite queer. Reckon that's what the marshal wants to be talkin' about."

2

John Locke stared at the deputy's smirking face. Ford was enjoying his moment, making the most of it. His small, dark eyes slid over the spectators lounging at the bar.

"That doesn't make any sense," Locke said.

The deputy shrugged. "Maybe it does and again, maybe it don't. Ain't for me to say. Any talkin' you want to do you'll have to do to the marshal. Come on, let's go."

They walked through the silent saloon, out into the street. Locke hesitated long enough to take up the reins of the bay and then turned for the jail. He anchored the big horse at the rail and with Luke Ford slouching at his heels, entered the marshal's office.

Several men had gathered there. Hazen Carey, looking much older; Frank Chance, Fred Dean, the Reverend Mr. Strickland, minister of the Christian Church; three

17

other men unknown to Locke but apparently leaders also in the town.

Dean and Chance nodded gravely to Locke and extended their hands in welcome. He accepted them and immediately placed his attention on Hazen Carey.

"Like to straighten this out quick, marshal. Got a long ride ahead of me and can't afford to lose any time."

Luke Ford dropped Locke's pistol onto the desk with a loud clatter. "Claims he was just ridin' through. Appears to me he's in a mighty big rush."

Carey glanced at the weapon and then at his deputy. "I'd say you are a lucky man, Luke." He moved around to his scarred, swivel chair and settled into it slowly. The Reverend Mr. Strickland and the men unknown to Locke nodded and filed out silently.

Dean said, "Where you headed, Johnny?"

"Got a good job waiting for me up in Wyoming. Foreman on the Walking W spread. Supposed to have been there a week ago. I lose much more time, they won't hold up for me."

Hazen Carey stared moodily at Locke. "You got any proof of that?"

Locke returned the lawman's gaze. "I need some?"

"You want to get out of here in a hurry. A letter or something like that, backing up what you say, would sure help."

Locke said, "Got nothing on me. Guess you could check with the Walking W people."

"Take four or five days," Dean observed.

Anger began to stir again through John Locke. "Your deputy tells me you think I had something to do with a holdup and shooting this morning. That right?"

Carey said, "That's what you're here for."

"Like I told him, I just rode in off the trail —"

"You prove that? You prove where you were last night and early this morning?"

"Camped along the river —"

"Anybody see you there?"

Locke shook his head. "Was alone. Don't recall seeing anybody pass by. But you're barking up the wrong tree if you think I had anything to do with it! Or that Bert or Starr Whitcomb did either."

"You're mighty sure about them," the marshal said. "Especially when the driver said he recognized them both. Also said the guard plugged one of them when they rode off."

"He was wrong," Locke replied doggedly. "The Whitcombs aren't outlaws."

Frank Chance drew a cigar from his vest pocket, lit it. "This the first time you been around since you left here?"

Locke said, "First time."

"Reckon things have changed some," the saloonman drawled and blew a cloud of blue smoke into the stale air.

Carey rose and walked to the window. He glanced out into the street. "Taking that posse long enough," he grumbled.

"They're waitin' on Beahm and his men," Ford explained.

"Somebody said he was havin' a time findin' Morgan and Tilton."

"We could do without them," the lawman said. "And Beahm better be showing up if he wants to go with us. No need of it, anyway. I figure I can handle this without any help from the stage line's investigator." He swung about suddenly and faced Locke. "What did you say brought you here this morning?"

"Was riding through. Figured on passing the time of day here with Fred Dean and then the Whitcombs. Like I said, I'm late and planned on moving right along."

"You claim you were in an all-fired hurry and that you were going to say howdy to Fred here and the Whitcomb boys and nobody else — yet Luke found you killing time in Frank Chance's place, having a drink. Don't jibe."

Locke moved his shoulders in exasperation. "Just took a notion to have a beer. And I've known Frank a long time."

"You right sure you haven't seen the Whitcombs — not for five years?"

"I haven't."

"Marshal, seems to me," Fred Dean began but Carey waved him into silence.

"Seems strange to me," he said, moving up nearer to Locke, "you're showing up here this particular morning, the same day the stage is held up and robbed by the Whitcombs and two other men. Maybe even more. Now, you grew up with the Whitcombs, just about the same as blood kin, I'd say. And you got yourself a reputation as a fast gun. All adds up as mighty queer —"

"Not at all," Locke replied evenly. "First place, I don't believe it was the Whitcombs that driver saw. He made a mistake. They wouldn't be mixed up in any holdup. And as for me just happening to ride through, what's odd about that? I rode through another town yesterday and some others before that." He stopped, waited out a long minute. "And about my gun — you ever see a wanted dodger on me?"

"Nope, reckon I never have."

"Then there's no reason to bring that in. I never yet drew it except to protect myself."

Carey shrugged. "That's the story on every outlaw. There's always a first time."

"Here comes Beahm," Frank Chance said.

Silence fell across the small, heat-packed room. Beahm, a large man, heavily built and with sharp, black eyes, a hard mouth and prominent nose, pushed into the office. He was followed closely by two men, a red-headed younger cowboy and one about his own age.

"Well, marshal, you ready to ride?"

"Been ready," Carey said shortly. "Was waiting on you."

Beahm glanced at Locke. "Who's this? Don't recollect seeing him before around here."

"Name of Locke. Grew up with the Whitcomb boys. Says he was just dropping by to say howdy, after five years."

Beahm studied Locke through narrowed lids. "Sort of funny, you picking this particular morning," he said, echoing Carey's observation.

Locke returned his glance coolly. "I don't know you, mister. So keep out of this."

"He can't," Hazen Carey spoke up. "He's Matt Beahm, special investigator for the Dangerfield stage people. Just happened to be in this part of the country looking into these holdups. Men with him work for him. The redhead is Tilton. Other one is Morgan."

Locke took a closer look at Morgan. Something about the man was familiar but he could not place him exactly. He was thinking of another thing that moment, anyway; something the marshal had just said.

"There's been some more holdups around here?"

Carey said, "Three."

"And nobody figured it was the Whitcombs pulling them?"

The lawman said, "No. Guess not."

"Now, all of a sudden they've turned outlaws!" Locke's voice was heavy with scorn. "And because I happen to know them, I'm an outlaw, too! Marshal, you don't make much sense."

Beahm snorted. "No matter what this ridgerunner says, it was the Whitcombs. That driver said he recognized them both. Don't see as we need any more proof." He stopped, swiveled his attention to Carey. "You figure he's got something to do with it?"

The lawman said, "Could have."

"You think I would have come riding into

town if I did?" Locke demanded.

"Be a smart move," Carey replied. "You could have figured nobody would give you a second thought. You could find out what we planned to do and then tip off the Whitcombs."

John Locke shrugged in disgust. It was like ramming his head against a wall. He could get nowhere and the idea that he or the Whitcombs could have had anything to do with the holdups and shooting was ridiculous.

"Well, make up your mind what you're going to do with this ridgerunner," Beahm said, using the derisive term again for Locke. "Let's get underway. Longer we wait the harder it's going to be to track those outlaws down."

"Just what I was saying earlier," Carey retorted, "when we were waiting for you."

The investigator favored Carey with a slow glance. It was plain he thought little of the old lawman's ability, only tolerated him it would appear because of his legal authority in the matter. He said, "Well, we're ready now, marshal."

Luke Ford swung to Carey. "What you want me to do with Locke? Turn him loose?"

The lawman shook his head. "No. Put him

in a cell. Figure it might be a smart idea to keep him around for a spell. At least, until we get to the bottom of this."

Anger swelled through Locke. "Now, wait a minute, marshal! You can't do this! You've got to have a reason to hold me."

"I admit it," Carey said blandly, putting on his wide-brimmed hat. "And I got them."

"What charge?"

"No special charge. Only that you're one of the Whitcombs and I figure that's enough to hold on to you. Let's call it suspicion. Now, if we catch up with the outlaws and find out they aren't the Whitcomb boys, like we figure, you've got some proving to do and I think it will be a heap easier, having you handy, to do that."

"This can cost me my job," Locke said, striving to keep the fury from his voice. "I've got no time to hang around here, I've got to get to Wyoming."

Beahm chuckled. "We'll write you a letter, friend," he said.

Carey said nothing. He motioned for Luke Ford. The deputy stepped forward, took Locke by the arm and shoved him toward the open door of a cell. Locke shook the man's arm off angrily. He came around, his arms half lifted, rock hard fists clenched.

Ford, gun in hand, grinned at him. "Go

25

ahead," he invited softly. "Just you start somethin'. Been hopin' you would. Like a chance to square up with you."

Locke paused, frowned. "Square up with me? For what?"

Ford kept his voice low. "A lot of things. You and Bert Whitcomb always thought you was such big shakes. Always actin' like you owned the whole country."

Locke stared at the man. "That was a long time ago, Luke. Can't remember us ever doing anything to hurt you."

"You wouldn't," the deputy replied. "You was always so high and mighty you couldn't notice —"

"How about it, Luke?" Carey's voice broke in from the adjoining room.

"Inside," Ford said, motioning to the cell with his gun. "Hate to have to shoot a big man like you Locke, but don't think I wouldn't enjoy it! All I need is a reason."

"I can believe that," Locke replied and walked into the barred cubicle. He watched Ford slam the door, turn the lock.

The marshal appeared in the doorway. He walked to the cell. "Sorry I got to do this to you, son, but I reckon I don't have much choice. If you've got nothing to do with that holdup, you'll be out of here and on your way right soon."

"Meaning when?"

"Couple of days. Three at the most."

Locke swore. "Marshal, I can't lose that much time! I've got to get on the trail. I can't afford to lose that job."

Carey shrugged. "Like I say, I'm sorry. But it can't be helped. I've got the law to look after. With a little luck, I might be able to turn you loose tonight."

"Luck?"

"We get our hands on those outlaws first off, I'll know what to do about you."

The lawman turned away. "Luke," he called out. "You stick around here close."

A few moments after that Locke saw him and Beahm, with their posse, ride off down the street.

3

For a long time John Locke stared through the barred window while a dull sort of anger throbbed steadily through him. It was unbelievable! He had intended only to pause in Three Forks for a brief time, long enough to renew acquaintances and then be on his way to keep what he figured to be the most important appointment in his life. And now, here he was locked in a cell, suspected, if not actually accused, of holdup and murder!

It could cost him that coveted job as foreman, he realized soberly. Even if he could overcome the lateness with some explanation, the fact that he had been held in jail and was a suspect in a serious crime would work against him. The Walking W was owned by a foreign syndicate and managed by a group of eastern lawyers. They would go strictly by the book and anyone even remotely connected with criminal activity would receive little consideration from them.

He wheeled about and stalked to the front of the cell. Through the doorway he could see Luke Ford sitting at Carey's desk, his feet hooked over an open drawer.

"Deputy!" he called. "How about some writing stuff? Paper and a pencil. And an envelope."

Ford rose lazily and sauntered to the front of the cell. He looked Locke over speculatively. "What for?"

"Write a letter, what else would I want it for?" Locke snapped, temper pushing him hard. "Been a long time working up to that job in Wyoming and I stand a good chance of losing it if I don't show up pretty soon. Figure maybe a letter might save it for me — at least fix it so I can explain what happened."

Ford shrugged. "Don't see why you're so anxious to take that kind of a job. Way I hear it, you could hire out that gun of yours for a lot of money, any time you wanted to."

Locke returned the deputy's insolent gaze. "Don't know what you've been hearing, or where, but my gun's not for hire. Never has been."

"Sure, sure. And I reckon you got that fast iron reputation from shootin' whiskey bottles off a fence rail."

Locke made no reply. He waited out a minute and then said, "What about the pencil and paper?"

Ford shook his head. "You'd better wait and talk to the marshal about that. Might be he don't want you writin' letters. Anyway, I ain't got the authority —"

"Authority! You need authority to give me a piece of paper and a pencil?"

Locke halted his angry words abruptly. A girl had entered the office, coming in from the street. She hesitated just inside the doorway, glanced about. John Locke recognized her immediately. It was Sally. She looked much the same as he remembered her; no older, a bit heavier which added to her beauty. But time had blurred his memory of her some. He had not recalled her hair being so dark or her brown eyes so large and soft. The old feeling swept through him again, filling him with its vast loneliness and he knew in that moment he would never get her out of his blood. It was an impossible, hopeless task.

The deputy turned, saw her. He walked back into the main office. "You wantin' somethin', Sally? Your pa ain't around here now. He left."

The girl shook her head. Sunlight glinted

off the dark folds of her hair. "I'd like to talk to Johnny, Luke."

The deputy glanced quickly at Locke. "By jeebies, that's right! I'd about forgot you two was mighty close friends once."

"Still are, I hope," Sally replied in a low voice.

Ford pondered for a moment. "Reckon there's no reason why the prisoner can't have you for a visitor. You ain't carryin' no concealed weapon, are you?" he added with a grin.

Sally said patiently, "No, no weapon, Luke."

Ford stepped aside and the girl walked slowly into the cell area. She met Locke's gaze with an uncertain smile upon her softly curved lips.

"Hello, Johnny."

Locke nodded. "How are you, Sally?"

She moved up to the bars, half turned to glance at Luke Ford. He still stood in the doorway, watching intently. When she faced him, he shrugged, sauntered off. She came back to Locke at once.

"Oh, Johnny, I'm so glad to see you!" she exclaimed, her features taut with worry.

"How did you know I was here? Your pa?"

She said, "Yes. He told me they were hold-ing you. They think you had something to do with that holdup and the murders."

Locke said, "Well, I didn't have — no more than Bert or Starr! What's the matter with people around here, anyway?"

She searched his dark, wind-burned face closely. "Things have changed since you went away, Johnny. So very much!"

"I believe it!" Locke said with conviction.

"All these holdups and shootings, everybody's on edge."

"They must be to think like they do. But nobody will ever make me believe the Whitcombs were in on any of it. I know them too well. I don't give a rap what that driver said."

Sally glanced down. In a low voice she said. "It's not like it used to be. They've changed, too, terribly. Especially Bert."

"How do you mean? You sound almost like you might suspect them, too. Why would they want to hold up a stage, or anything else?"

"After you left, things went bad at the ranch," the girl said. She halted, looked again toward Luke Ford. He was leaning against the doorframe of the outer office, his back to them as he watched something on the street.

"Their herd caught anthrax. Bert and Starr lost everything they had. Then there was a fire that destroyed the barn and a lot of feed they had stored away. Everything just seemed to go wrong for them.

"Bert took to drinking and running around with a couple of hard cases that used to hang around town. I guess Starr tried to keep things going but Bert didn't pay much mind to him."

Sally moved her hands in a gesture of hopelessness. "I don't know what I think! But you don't know Bert Whitcomb as he is now! He's different, someone else altogether. He's not the Bert you knew five years ago!"

"Always was a little wild and crazy maybe, but nothing bad," Locke said absently. "He was a great one for fun."

"That's the way you remember him. But it's different now. Johnny, I'm afraid — I'm almost afraid to think — and if they catch up to him, there will be a lynching sure!"

Locke had no immediate reply to that. He only stared at the girl, finding it hard to believe what she was telling him. Bert and Starr Whitcomb — outlaws, killers? Sally would not say it but he knew she believed it.

He said, "Hard to think they'd get themselves mixed up in something like this. But,

33

you being Bert's wife, you ought to know
—"

"I'm not Bert's wife," she cut in quickly.
"We never got married."

Surprise blanked his features. "You didn't?
But when I left you were making plans —"

"I know what we planned," she said in a
calm voice. "But we called it off. Or rather,
Bert did when things all went wrong at the
ranch. He insisted we postpone everything.
Said he wouldn't take a wife while he was
broke.

"It hurt a little at first but not as much as
I thought it would. And his being broke
didn't have anything to do with the way I
felt. I would have married him if all he
owned was the shirt on his back. But Bert
has a sort of pride you can't get around, so
we put it off."

Locke said, "That was five years ago!
Must have been a few times between then
and now when you could have got together
and gone through with it."

"I suppose there were but Bert never
mentioned it to me after that and I just
stopped thinking about it. I guess now it
was all for the best."

He glanced at her sharply. "Meaning?"

"Maybe it was a mistake from the start. I
think I sort of realized that the day I

watched you ride out."

John Locke considered her words thoughtfully. He believed he understood their deeper meaning. But it was too much to hope for and he would not permit himself to accept it. Not just yet, anyway. However, there was no denying the gladness that had risen within him.

He reached through the bars, touched her downcast face and tipped it up to meet his. "You think Bert and Starr did it, don't you?"

"I don't know what to think," she replied truthfully. "I'm afraid it's true — yet I won't let myself believe it."

"Sort of the way I feel now, I reckon," he said. "When they first told me they suspected them, I thought they were loco and told them so. Now, after what you've told me, I'm not so dead sure. But I'll still have to know it first hand. I'll take nobody else's word for it."

Sally looked away. "It's something we may never find out for sure. Papa says that if they catch Bert and Starr, a lynch mob will hang them before they ever reach town. People around here have made up their minds they did it and because both the guard and the driver lived here they're going to take things into their own hands."

John Locke studied the girl's torn, worried features. He wondered how deep her feelings went; if it was no more than the normal anxiety any woman would feel for an old friend threatened with violent death — or did she yet love him as once she had.

The situation clarified itself in Locke's mind in that next moment. It was something he must know to satisfy — or still — forever the hope that had sprung again into his heart. And there were other reasons; his own desire to know the truth, to help Bert and Starr and prevent a lynching if such was in the background. And there was the sense of deep obligation he felt he owed the Whitcomb family itself. Tom Whitcomb and his wife had taken him in, an orphan, and raised him as one of their own. The least he could do would be to stand by their sons in time of trouble and see that they received a fair deal.

He looked beyond the girl to Luke Ford, still standing in the doorway. He said quietly, "Guess there's only one thing to do, find Bert and Starr and straighten this all out."

She looked up quickly. "But here in jail — how can you do anything —"

He grinned. "Always some way to get out of a place like this, if you need to. Now, you go along and don't fret about anything. Just stick around your pa's store so I'll know where to find you. And, one thing more — don't say anything to anybody."

She nodded, smiled hopefully. "All right, Johnny. But be careful. I don't think I —"

"Don't be worrying about me," he cut in.

"Good-bye," she murmured and turned away.

4

Deputy Luke Ford remained in the doorway for several moments, watching Sally Dean walk slowly off toward her father's store. Someone else strolled by, spoke, the man's hard boot heels rapping loudly on the board sidewalk. Back, down the street, a blacksmith rang his anvil and in the alley behind the jail a dog barked in a steady, monotonous way. Finally, Ford turned, came back into the office. It was hot. He removed his hat, dropped it onto the marshal's desk, mopped at his sweaty forehead. He moved to the opening to where he could see Locke.

"You gettin' hungry?"

Locke said, "Am for a fact. You didn't give me time for breakfast. Could sure use some victuals." He realized it was near noon. A half a day already gone.

Ford grunted, returned to the front entrance. He stood in the doorway for a moment, keeping far enough within to avoid the sun. After a moment he caught the attention of someone across the street and shouted an order for two plates of food. That done, he wheeled about and sat down heavily in Hazen Carey's chair.

The meals arrived a few minutes later, brought by a short, squat man with a full, black mustache. He was a stranger to Locke. He placed the tray on the desk and stepped back expectantly.

"Marshal will pay you when he comes in," Ford said.

"For you, too?" the man asked in a doubtful voice.

"Mine, too. When I got to stay here and can't go out to eat, the town pays my fare." He pushed his finger into the thick stew on one of the plates, tasted it critically. He pointed to the coffee. "Little hot to be drinkin' that stuff. When you go back, holler at Pete Forbes to bring some beer."

The waiter frowned. "Won't see Pete, unless I walk clear down to Frank's place."

"Know that," the deputy said. "But I can't leave the prisoner. Marshal's orders."

"I can watch him," the man offered. "He can't do nothin' not inside that cell."

Ford wagged his head. "Nope, can't leave. You tell Pete, eh?"

The waiter shrugged and wheeled to the

doorway. Ford picked up one of the plates. He sat a cup of coffee on its edge, forcing it partly into the stew to steady it and carried it to Locke.

"Back in the corner," he ordered, halting at the barred gate.

Locke moved to the far side of the cell. The deputy produced his ring of keys, opened the grillwork. Watching Locke narrowly, he placed the food on the floor and hastily withdrew.

Locke was assessing his chances. It would have been a good time to rush the deputy when he opened the door. Both his hands were occupied at that moment. But there was the matter of the man, Pete, who would be bringing the beer. It would be better to wait.

He allowed Ford to lock the door and then picked up his plate. He sat down on the edge of the cot and began to eat. He was not particularly hungry despite the fact he had missed an early morning meal. The coffee tasted good but he drank sparingly of it. The bartender, Pete, showed up at that point bringing not one but two glasses of brew. Ford did not offer one to Locke but accepted the error and claimed both mugs for himself.

Locke finished his meal. He placed his

empty plate on the floor and settled back on the cot to roll himself a smoke. The partly full cup of coffee was beside him. A plan had formed in his mind, one that might work and permit him to escape, if his timing was right. He begrudged each passing minute but he was careful not to show it. He could not afford to arouse any suspicions in the deputy. Keeping his movements leisurely, he completed his cigarette and stretched out on the cot.

He watched Ford covertly. He saw him scrape up the last of his stew, mop the plate thoroughly with a scrap of bread. He drained both glasses of beer and topped that off with the last of his coffee. He belched, swung about in the marshal's chair and glared at Locke.

"You done?"

Locke said, "All done."

Ford rose, came into the cell room. He glanced critically at Locke's sprawled shape and then opened the door. He knelt down to take up the plate, then paused.

"Where's the cup?"

Locke said, "Oh — right here."

He sat up, reached for the near full container. He started to hand it to the man and then, with one, quick motion, flung it into his eyes. Ford, off balance, fell backwards.

41

At that same fragment of time, Locke lunged. He struck the deputy straight on, his knees driving with brutal force into Ford's body. Both men went down in a heap. Locke knew he must make it fast and quietly. A shout from the deputy could easily be heard on the street and bring aid immediately.

He spun quickly, gathered his knees beneath himself. He grabbed the lawman by the shirtfront, dragged him half upright with his left hand. With the right he drove a hard blow to the man's unprotected jaw. Ford grunted and went slack.

Locke allowed him to sink to the floor. He stepped hurriedly across the room to the marshal's desk. He found his gun in the second drawer, dropped it into the holster. He glanced toward the doorway. No one had heard the scuffling. He started to turn, to drag Ford into the cell he himself had so lately occupied and lock the door. In that moment he felt the deputy's arms go about his legs, tripping him. He went down, cursing his own carelessness. Ford had not been knocked out — at least, not hard enough.

Flat on his back he scrambled to get away from the deputy. Ford had hurled himself across his legs, pinning him down. He struck out at the man's sweaty face, missed.

Ford was trying to hold him down, keep him prone while he got his hands on his gun. Locke struck out again. This time he felt his knuckles drive into the man's flesh. It stalled Ford only momentarily. And then the deputy's fingers clamped down upon his throat.

He threw all his strength into an effort to dislodge Ford but the man's solid weight lay upon him and he had his legs spread in such a manner as to prevent himself from being rolled off. Locke's breath began to drag, to close off. His head suddenly was tight, seemed ready to burst. Through the harsh sounds of gasping and grunting he heard Ford mutter.

"Think . . . you can . . . get away from me. . . . Not . . . by a damn sight!"

The stains on the ceiling began to swim before John Locke's eyes. A faint mist hovered about the edges of his vision. He shook his head, seeking to throw off the cloudiness but the fingers entwined in his hair pinned him down, the hand clutching his throat held him almost motionless. Strength was ebbing from his long body. A sort of desperation seized him. He had only seconds left in which to act — if he were to act at all.

Summoning all his reserve he gathered his

legs beneath him. Then, with every ounce of power in his frame, he drove them upward. His knees dug sharply into Ford's belly. The deputy grunted in pain. He lurched forward over Locke. His fingers lost their grip on Locke's throat. He went on, head first, to the floor.

Locke twisted away from beneath the lawman's threshing legs. He rolled over, clawing at the man's shoulder. He saw Ford jerk away, saw the dull glint of metal in his hand as he came up with his pistol. It had shaken loose of its holster and dropped to the floor. Locke had a glimpse of the deputy's distorted face, wild with a killing fury.

He struck out with his left hand, batted the gun away. With his right he drew his own weapon, jammed it into Ford's backbone. He could have pulled the trigger, ended the fight immediately. He knew the shot, muffled by such close quarters, would likely go unnoticed along the street.

But his finger did not tighten about the trigger. There was no need to kill and John Locke, despite his reputation, had never shot a man except as a last resort in a matter of self defense.

"Drop it!" he grated into Ford's ear.

The deputy allowed the gun to clatter to the floor. Locke, heaving for breath, got to his knees. He moved warily around the lawman, picked up the fallen weapon. He skated it into a far corner of the room, and stood up.

"One yell," he promised in a low voice, "and you're dead."

Ford partly turned his head. "Maybe. I don't figure you'd pull that trigger. The shot would bring half the people in town up here."

"Sure," Locke said coolly, "but you wouldn't be alive to see them. And chances are I'd still get away with no trouble. Now, I'd like to leave here with you still breathing but you try to stop me again and I'll blow your head off! You understand me?"

Ford made no reply. Locke prompted him vigorously with the toe of his boot.

"I understand," the deputy grumbled.

"Then crawl into that cell. Stay on your hands and knees. I'll be right behind you."

The deputy did as he was directed. He halted in the center of the barred square. Locke picked up a pair of manacles from Carey's desk. He ordered Ford to rise and hold his hands behind his back. This done, he snapped the cuffs into place. He took the man's bandana and fashioned an effective gag. Finished, he stepped back, examined the lawman critically. Satisfied all was secure, he pushed him onto the cot.

"That ought to give me a little time," he said and moved out of the cell. He closed the heavy door, locked it. He then dropped the key into the side pocket of a brush jacket hanging on a wall peg. That should provide a few more additional minutes.

He pulled the inner panel shut behind him when he walked into the main office area, thus preventing any passerby, who might glance into the building, from seeing Ford in the cell. He stepped to the front entrance of the building. The bay still waited patiently at the hitching rail. Locke glanced about. In the hot, midday sunlight the street was deserted. He drew on his hat, stepped casually into the open. He walked slowly to the bay, pulled the reins free. He swung to the saddle, again taking a swift survey of the dusty canyon between the twin row of buildings. No one was in sight. So far, so good.

5

The man's inborn caution would not let him press his luck too far. His departure was going unnoticed, true enough, but to stay out in full view on Three Forks' main street would be unwise. Accordingly he followed its dusty length only for a short distance to a passageway which separated the jail from an adjoining structure, an abandoned saloon. He turned into that narrow corridor. He could hear the muffled thumpings of Deputy Ford as he pounded against the wall of his cell, endeavoring to attract someone's attention. Locke grinned. Likely it would be some time before the lawman aroused anyone's interest.

He came out behind the jail into an alley which traced an irregular course along the rear of other buildings that faced the street. An old man was in view a dozen yards down, dozing in a chair at the back of some sort of shop. Locke kept the bay at a slow, quiet walk. It was necessary that he pass the man, since his destination lay to the north, beyond the town. He had hoped he could make the cross over without being seen. It would simplify matters greatly if the marshal and his men, returning and finding him gone and thinking of search, could not be sure if he were still in the area or had ridden on to keep his appointment in Wyoming.

Which is what he should do, he told himself. He should be thinking of himself, of his own future. But he knew his conscience would never let him rest if he failed to do what he could for the Whitcombs — and for Sally Dean.

He swung the bay as far wide of the sleeping oldster as possible. He crossed in front of him, watching him narrowly as he did so. He was relieved to see the man remained quiet, apparently undisturbed by the passage of a rider. He met one more resident of Three Forks, a small boy, just as he reached the outskirts of the town. The boy paid him small attention and he gave him no more thought.

He heaved a sigh. He had managed to get beyond the buildings unchallenged, likely unseen and that was as he had hoped. The road which led to the Whitcomb place lay before him now, well-defined tracks that carved a route through the low, short hills toward the towering Blackfoot Mountains to the northwest.

The Whitcomb ranch lay near the foot of that range and to John Locke it was logical that he would find the Whitcomb brothers, guilty or not, in that area. As boys they had all roamed the high, cloud-capped country and knew well every deep canyon and long ridge that would offer them excellent hiding facilities. Most likely, if they sought to remain out of the clutches of Hazen Carey and his posse, they would make for the cabin in Catamount Canyon. It was a secret rendezvous they had used as youngsters and, in later years, employed as a base camp for deer hunting.

Of course, that all could have changed in five years. The cabin might be gone, could have fallen into decay or possibly burned to the ground during one of the severe electrical storms that periodically struck the Blackfoot country and scarred it with smoking fury. But to John Locke it was his best possibility. If the Whitcombs were not around the ranch itself, they would likely be holed up in the cabin.

The road forked, one branch keeping to the right, leading on eastward. The other swung to the left. Locke turned the bay onto the latter, seeing now and then some of the old landmarks that were familiar to him. An hour later he reached the south marker of the Whitcomb property, a stone cairn erected by Starr, Bert and himself when they were scarcely large enough to gather and carry the necessary rocks. In the center of the pile Tom Whitcomb had placed an iron rod, notching it with a file in a manner of his own design. Similar markers designated the remaining three corners of the ranch which sprawled for miles along the base of the mountains.

The country looked good to John Locke despite the lateness of the summer. Grass was plentiful although dry from summer's heat and he had a moment's keen regret that the fine ranch Tom Whitcomb had labored so hard to build for his sons had fallen into such neglect and disuse. But a man can never see into a definite future; he can only plan and hope things turn out the way he expects.

Timber began to thicken at that point of the range and toward a solid stand of brush, a quarter mile to his left, John Locke headed the bay. He was drawing near the ranch itself now and it would be unwise to ride out in the open. Marshal Hazen Carey and his men would be working the country, he was certain, and he might be seen.

He reached the band of brush which had offered such good rabbit hunting for the Whitcombs and himself in years gone by and sliced across it at a long tangent. His plan was to intercept and follow a path they once had used in reaching the ranch. He never located it and eventually realized the growing brush had swallowed it up when it was no longer followed by anyone.

It made no particular difference except to slow the bay's progress somewhat. It was now necessary to pick a route through the thick, tangled growth of tamarack and scrub oak. In the end he was glad there had been no open pathway and was thankful for the cover of the brush. When he was within a mile of the ranch house he became suddenly aware of voices — men's voices.

He halted abruptly, glanced about for a place in which he could hide. It sounded like several men, all moving toward him. He swung the bay around and walked him softly to one side, pulled up behind a thick stand of Osage orange. Several minutes later the riders broke into view. Three men; the investigator Mathew Beahm and his two helpers, Tilton and Morgan.

Beahm's dark face was grim with anger,

his voice deep and harsh. "Mighty strange to me that a dozen men ain't been able to turn up these Whitcombs! We know they rode back here after the holdup and we know somebody in the bunch was shot up bad. Now, one of you tell me just where the hell they could have gone."

Neither of the two assistants offered a reply. Beahm spat angrily. "You don't reckon it could be that the marshal and his men don't want us to find them, do you? The Whitcombs being from around here and so on."

Tilton, the red-haired man shook his head. "No, I don't figure it's that. Way it sounds to me them Whitcombs ain't so well liked."

"That's plumb sure," Morgan added. "That stage driver was pretty well thought of in town. I figure once we do get our hands on the Whitcombs, the marshal will never get them to jail. Not the way the town feels about it."

Beahm muttered something in low breath that Locke did not hear. He watched them draw nearer while a prickling began to crawl along his scalp. They were coming straight for the stand of brush in which he had taken refuge. He took a deep breath, dropped his hand to the gun at his hip. Beahm and his two men halted, pulled up in a small clearing only yards away. They ranged about in a half-circle, facing him. Beahm stared directly at the point where Locke had hidden.

Tension began to mount within Locke. Beahm did not see him, he was certain of that, but the slightest move on the part of the bay would instantly draw the investigator's attention. He remained frozen in the saddle, ready to fight if need be but praying it would not come to that yet.

Beahm said, "Well, it's sure mighty strange. They're bound to be around here somewhere."

Morgan stirred in the saddle. "You don't reckon the marshal's got any ideas —"

Beahm cut him off quickly. "No, I don't figure he does. And don't be talking it out loud. There's other men moving around in these trees. You could get heard."

Tilton said, "There's a hundred canyons along this side of the mountains. They could have ducked into any one of them. We could hunt for a month and not jump them because they would be movin' all the time."

"Any chance they'd double back to the ranch house?"

"Doubt that, Carey left two men there to watch out. They show up, they'll get nailed for sure."

"They're too smart for that," Beahm observed.

That was information that aided John Locke. Now he would not have to waste time riding to the ranch to see if Starr and Bert were there. And listening to the stage coach company investigator and his two men revealed something else; the Whitcomb brothers were definitely hiding out. Whether from a fear of lynch law, despite their actual innocence of the crime, or because they were involved in the holdup and killing, there was no way of knowing.

Beahm said, "Those canyons along the hills you were talking about — anybody working them now?"

"Carey himself, along with a few others. Guess the marshal figured they most likely would head for there."

"Looks to me like we'd all better ride over that way," Beahm said. "We sure ain't finding nothing around here." He lifted the reins of his horse, started to pull away and halted. "Tell you what I'll do," he said. "You boys stay on this job hard. You find that money for me and I'll split a thousand dollars special reward between you. That's five hundred a piece."

Tilton and Morgan came up sharply. "That go for just us or the rest of the posse in on it, too?" Tilton asked.

"I'm talking just to you two. I figure the pair of you working together can do a better job than all that posse wrapped up in a lump. Way I look at it, the marshal and his men are real interested in getting their hands on the outlaws. Me, I'm looking for the money."

Morgan studied Beahm throughtfully: "Meaning you don't care nothin' about catchin' up with the Whitcombs, so long as you find the money?"

Beahm glanced about. He nodded. "Meaning exactly that. All I want is the money — for the company, of course. They can string up the Whitcombs or roast them over a fire. Makes no difference to me."

"Supposin' we find them and they got the money on them. We hold them for the marshal and —"

"Forget the marshal," Beahm said softly. "You got guns, use them. Then bring me the money."

Tilton and Morgan exchanged glances. The red-headed cowboy said, "You got a deal, Mister Beahm."

"Then, let's get started."

John Locke watched the three men wheel about and strike westward for the Blackfoot Range. Beahm's words echoed strangely through his mind. It was an unusual attitude for a stage line man to take — and a cold one. It was almost as if he cared nothing about the apprehension of the outlaws, was interested only in recovering the money. Generally, a company did everything possible to stop masked bandits from preying upon their coaches. But perhaps there was a reason behind Beahm's actions. He should know what he was doing. One thing was certain, he had just signed a death warrant for Starr and Bert so far as the two men who worked for him were concerned.

The Whitcombs must be warned. If they were innocent and planned to turn themselves in, they must do so only to Hazen Carey. Tilton's suggestion that the canyons along the mountains being the most likely place for Bert and Starr to hide out was all too accurate. Locke realized he would have to move and move fast. Men combing the area would eventually stumble upon the shack in Catamount Canyon. He would have to get there first.

He waited another minute until he could no longer hear the sounds of passage of Beahm and his companions and then pulled away from the brush behind which he had hidden. He headed the bay straight for the southern end of the mountains, figuring that route would keep him farthest away from the posse and Beahm and eventually bring him out at a point near the cabin.

He kept the gelding at a fairly good pace through the brush for a quarter of a mile. The thought occurred to him that, at such speed, it should not take long to reach the canyon. He would be well ahead of the others. And then the loud snapping of a dry branch brought him up short. He looked about quickly, searching for a place into which he could move but saw none. He was out in the open, near the center of a small clearing. It was too late to change his position.

He dropped his right hand to his gun, drew it. With his left he gently rubbed the bay's neck, hoping to quiet the big horse. He rode out the dragging moments, not knowing from which direction danger might come. The crackling sound had been clear and plain but the exact point where it had originated was difficult to determine.

He saw the rider then. One man on a gray horse a few yards off to the right. He was pointing for the mountains, his face turned partly away, eyes looking ahead. The bay lifted his ears at the sight of the gray. Locke immediately touched him lightly with his spurs, swung him off to the left. Better to risk motion than permit the gelding to nicker or shake his head and set up a jingle of bridle metal. He kept his eyes on the posse member. He continued on. He had not noticed the man and horse in the clearing.

Locke took a deep breath. That had been a close call. He would have to proceed with more caution, which in turn, meant less haste. This would jeopardize the possibility of his arriving at the mountains ahead of the others. But better to be late than fall into the hands of the posse and never get there at all.

He swung the bay into a long and narrow lane between two rows of trees. Quite suddenly the gelding shied violently, halted. Locke's hand again was on his gun. He threw his glance ahead into the deep shadows. A horse stood just beyond a clump of brush, a chunky little buckskin. It's head hung in exhaustion. The saddle was empty.

Locke, drawing his weapon, dismounted quickly. He walked forward a few steps. The dark shape of a man lay off to one side of the trail. The back of his gray shirt was stained with blood. Locke stepped quickly to his side. Taking the fallen man by the shoulder, he turned him over gently. A groan escaped the wounded rider's lips.

Locke stared at the tortured features looking up at him.

It was Starr Whitcomb.

6

Whitcomb opened his eyes with great effort. The change in his old friend was a solid shock to John Locke. His features were broader, coarser and heavily lined. Now, with the lusterless pallor of death lying across them, he appeared to be many years older than he actually was. He looked up at Locke, wonder coming into his eyes. He endeavored to pull himself to one elbow but failed. He had not the strength left in his body and settled back.

"Johnny," he muttered in a disbelieving sort of way. "Johnny Locke."

Locke laid him out flat on the smooth floor of the forest. He turned to the bay, unhooked his canteen and hurried back to Whitcomb. Removing the cap of the container, he lifted Starr's head and poured a swallow of water between the wounded man's colorless lips.

Whitcomb choked momentarily and again

opened his eyes. He grinned weakly. "Whiskey . . . in my saddlebags," he muttered.

Locke hastened to the buckskin. He found the half-empty bottle of liquor at once and returned to the side of his friend. Starr drank deeply from the bottle, turned his head aside to signify he had enough. Whitcomb had lost a great deal of blood and was very weak. One glance at the wound had told John Locke his friend had only a short time left.

"What I needed," Whitcomb said then, feeling the lifting effects of the whiskey. "Nothing like a stiff shot to keep a man going."

He tried again to raise himself but Locke pressed him back gently. "Don't move. You'll start the bleeding again."

Whitcomb lay back, studied Locke's face. "Last man I ever expected to see. You with that posse?"

Locke shook his head. "Matter of fact, I'm dodging them. Was looking for you and Bert."

Whitcomb considered that for a long moment. Then he asked, "Why?"

"Was just riding through and figured to stop off for a couple of hours. Heard then you and Bert were in a bit of trouble."

"Reckon you've heard about the holdup."

"Only that there had been one and the driver had said he recognized you and Bert. I figured he was wrong, had made a mistake. Guess now he knew what he was talking about."

"He knew," Starr Whitcomb replied and stirred uncomfortably. "Was Bert and me and a couple of other men."

The question leaped from John Locke's lips before he could halt it. "How the hell did you and Bert get mixed up in a thing like that?"

Starr managed a wry grin. "How does anything ever get started, Johnny? One thing sort of leads to another, like wading a horse out into quicksand. First thing you know it's too late to turn back. Then you're over your head and there's nothing you can do."

"But stage robbery — and murder! I wouldn't believe it when they told me. And they said there were other robberies before this one."

"Not by Bert and me. This was the first and, I reckon, my last. That guard's rifle bullet got me good." He looked straight into Locke's eyes as if hoping for some denial of his assumption. Seeing none there he sighed heavily.

"Never should have got mixed up in something like this. Not in my line and a man's crazy to start fooling around with a thing he don't know anything about. But I guess he don't always have a choice. How're things with you, Johnny? Doing all right?"

Locke nodded. "Riding north now to take on the job of ramrodding a good outfit." He stopped, looked closely at Whitcomb. He wished there was something he could do for his friend. But it was only a matter of minutes. The wound was a fatal one otherwise he would manage somehow to get Starr to a doctor.

He said, curious, "What do you mean by no choice?"

Starr moved impatiently, winced at the pain that shot through his body. He turned his eyes to the whiskey bottle still in Locke's hand. Locke gave him another deep drink which seemed to revive him considerably.

"No use bawlin' about it now. It was only a little problem I was having with Bert." He halted, cocked his head in that way Locke recalled so well and added, "You should never have pulled out, Johnny. Was a big mistake for all of us."

"Only thing I could do, knowing how Sally felt about Bert — and the way he felt about her."

"You were too close to Bert," Starr murmured. "You never could see his faults. I

63

don't figure he ever wanted that girl. He just plain didn't want you to have her."

Locke made no reply to that but the meaning of it drilled into him with a sickening intensity. After a time he said, "I saw Sally. Was surprised to hear they had never married. Said you'd had some bad luck at the ranch and went broke. She figures that's the reason Bert backed down and wouldn't go through with it."

Starr cleared his throat. A spasm shook his frame, distorted his pale features. He glanced again at the liquor. "Give me another shot of that, Johnny. Didn't used to care much for the stuff. Last couple of years it has come in right handy, however." He gulped down the fiery liquid noisily, almost emptying the bottle. "Reckon it's going to hold out just long enough," he said and grinned.

"You in a big hurry to reach that there job you were talking about?"

Locke shook his head slowly. Hours counted now, where the job was concerned, he knew. And each one lost lessened his chances. But he said, "No, got plenty of time, Starr."

Whitcomb said, "Fine. Got a little favor I'd like to ask of you, if I can. I ain't going to be around now to look after Bert and he sure is one that takes some looking after. Kept me hopping the last few years, trying to keep him headed straight and pulling him out of one scrape after another. None of it was ever real bad. Not until this stage holdup thing."

Locke said, "Maybe this is one time nobody can help him, Starr. Both those men that were shot up in the holdup died. It's a killing."

Whitcomb's eyes closed wearily. A gusty sigh passed through his lips. "Guess I always knew it would end up like this, someday. Just a sort of hunch. But I kept telling myself Bert wasn't all bad, only wild and headstrong. Was just fooling myself, that's what I was doing. Now it's gone too far and there's not much can be done. Should have run off those two hard cases he fell in with when they first turned up. I'm not crying but they're the ones who got us into this."

"The two outlaws that were with you in the holdup?"

"Yeh. Man named Gregg, Chino Gregg. Other one is called Nate Corrigan. Both bad ones. Killers."

"They with Bert now?"

"Meeting him at the old shack in the canyon. You know where. Place we used to play around in when we were kids. After the

65

holdup this morning we split up. Idea was to meet there this afternoon after the posse petered out."

Whitcomb caught the question in Locke's eyes. "Bert didn't know I'd stopped a bullet, else he would have stuck with me. We handed him the box with the money in it and told him to ride for it while Chino and Nate and one did the shooting. It was every man for himself. I ran out of luck."

"They're all fresh out of luck," Locke said. "The country is swarming with men looking for them. Not only Hazen Carey with a big posse but the investigator for the stage line with a couple of special deputies, too. They'll never make it." He could have mentioned the possibility of a lynch mob and the shoot-first instructions he had heard Beahm give his men but did not. There was no point in painting the picture any worse.

Starr coughed deeply. He grinned at Locke. "One more swallow in that bottle, Johnny? Guess I'd better have it. Things are getting dark."

Locke tipped the bottle to Whitcomb's mouth, watched as the man drained it to the last drop. Empty, he tossed it into the brush.

"That favor I mentioned . . . you think you might find the time . . ."

"Name it. I'll do what I can, Starr. You know that without even asking."

"Get to the shack. You'll have to hurry if you get there before Chino and Nate. See if you can talk Bert into turning over the money to the marshal before it's too late and giving himself up along with it. Maybe it won't go so hard on him, was he to do it before they catch him."

Starr paused, gathered his strength. "He didn't have anything to do with the shooting. Tell that to Carey for me. Bert had already left when that started. It was Chino and Nate and me using the guns. I don't know which one of us hit the driver and the guard but it sure wasn't Bert. He was already gone. He had the box with the money in it and was heading for the shack."

Whitcomb hesitated again. He was having trouble shaping his words, making them come out right and the effort was exacting a heavy toll from his faltering strength.

Locke said, "I'll do everything I can, Starr. When he learns you've been hit, maybe it will jar a little sense into him."

Starr nodded weakly. "You can talk him into it, was you to try. But look out for Gregg and Corrigan. They're bad, plenty bad. And they're not going to take kindly to losing their share of that money."

"Met their kind before. Don't worry about that part of it."

Whitcomb grinned. "That's good, Johnny. Figured you'd be able to handle it. You always were a dependable sort of a cuss . . . Johnny . . ."

Locke leaned closer to catch the man's trailing words. He could hear no sound of his breathing. He brushed aside the shirt fabric, laid his hand on Starr's chest. He could feel a slight heart beat, very slow and weak. A vast and terrible loneliness washed through him.

"Starr!" he said in a harsh voice.

Whitcomb opened his eyes, forced a half grin to his slack lips. " 'Bout my time, Johnny. Good . . . to see you again . . . You sure . . . never should have left, Johnny. You . . ."

The words faded off into silence. Locke felt again for that feeble pulse. It had ceased. Starr Whitcomb was dead.

7

John Locke stood by the side of his friend for several long minutes. In the deep hush of the forest, he was thinking back, remembering the days when they were small boys, and recalling the good things they had enjoyed. Starr had been the careful one, the one of restraint; the older brother looking out for the younger. And now, because of that, he was dead. He deserved a better end.

Soberly, he turned and caught up the buckskin. He had no liking for what he must do but there was no other answer. He would prefer to take Starr's body in to town himself, accompany it on that last journey. But there was no time for that now and Starr, if he were watching from some remote corner, would understand.

Locke lifted Whitcomb's body and draped it across the buckskin's saddle, anchoring it firmly so it would not slide off. That done, he paused again while bitter thoughts of what had come to pass moved through him once more. But it was too late for thinking, for helping or doing much of anything. He looped the reins of the buckskin over the horn and turned to his own horse. He mounted, and with the buckskin on a lead rope, he returned to the main trail. Heading the little horse with its lifeless rider toward Three Forks, he slapped him smartly and sent him on his way.

He sat, then, in the shade of a spreading cottonwood tree and considered his next move. He had learned what he had set forth to discover; it was true about the Whitcombs. They had turned outlaw. He had refused to believe it but now there was no doubt as he had heard it from Starr Whitcomb's own lips. For him, the matter should end here. Regardless of what Starr had said, there was little if anything at all he could do for Bert. He was as guilty, in the eyes of men and the law, as if he had held a gun in his hand and done the shooting himself. And he would have to pay the penalty for it. If he listened to Starr he would not be in such a position — and Starr would be alive.

Locke knew he should be on the road to Wyoming. Delaying longer could prove costly, but he was thinking of his promise to the dying Starr. He had said he would find

Bert, would do what he could to make him see things in their proper light. It was a bit late for that, he reflected again, yet Starr had wanted him to try. Therefore, he would. And there was also the matter of Sally Dean. That, too, must be resolved.

He glanced to the sun. Early afternoon. Starr had said they were all to meet eventually in the shack hidden in Catamount Canyon; that if he moved fast he might possibly get there ahead of Chino Gregg and the other gunman, Nate Corrigan. An hour had already drained away while he had been with Starr. Now, that possibility could have been lost. He shrugged his wide shoulders and wheeled the blaze-faced bay around. It didn't really matter. He had to see Bert, talk to him. He would just have to take his chances with Gregg and Corrigan. He could handle them if it became necessary. He put the gelding to a slow trot, headed for the lower end of the Blackfoot Range where Catamount Canyon lay.

He reached the mouth of that slash without interruption, which relieved him considerably. It could mean that Hazen Carey and Beahm, and all the other members of the posse who were working the slopes of the mountains, were still to the north. If true, he would have only Bert's outlaw friends to

71

contend with.

He turned up the narrow trail which led into the canyon, leaning forward in the saddle as he rode, to study the trail for hoof prints. There were a great number of them in the loose soil, indicating there had been much riding to and from the cabin in the last few days. All of which helped him little in those moments.

He allowed the bay to pick his own way slowly up the steepening path, thinking more of silence now than of speed. He checked back through his memory, recalling the shack, the lay of the surrounding terrain. It would be in a small clearing, fairly well hemmed in by trees and brush. He could make an unseen approach from any side, simply by swinging off the trail and taking to the brush. This he decided to do. If Bert and the outlaws were watching, their attention likely would be directed to the canyon's entrance.

He cut to his left, coming in upon the cabin from the west. He dismounted well back in the timber and made his way on foot to the edge of the clearing. There he halted. A lone horse stood before the shack which appeared to be in surprisingly good condition after so long a time. Evidently Starr and Bert had kept it in repair, even made some improvements. He remained there in the outskirts for three or four minutes, assuring himself there was no one else around except the rider of the solitary horse, whoever he might be, and then swiftly crossed the open ground to the low-roofed cabin.

The structure had a door and a single window. Locke went first to the smaller opening and peered through the dust covered, streaky glass. A sigh of thankfulness passed through Locke. It was Bert Whitcomb. He sat at the crude table alone; a different Bert Whitcomb than he had known five years previous, but the same. This one was much thinner, his face narrower and sharp but still with that certain dark handsomeness to it.

He now had a quick, nervous way about him, as if he expected trouble from every quarter and at any moment. Locke studied him for a time. He was in the process of removing the stolen money from the metal box in which it had been placed by the shipper. The currency, apparently destined for some bank, was arranged in neat packets which in turn had been placed in small, white canvas bags that bore the name of the stage coach line. A pair of saddlebags lay open nearby. There were no signs of the other outlaws.

Locke eased gently around to the open doorway. He did not know just what reaction he should expect from Bert Whitcomb. The man was in a highly nervous frame of mind and approaching him would have to be done with care. He halted just outside the opening. Whitcomb worked steadily at the table — a table he and Starr and Bert had built with lumber discarded from a tool shed, he recalled in that moment.

He stepped noiselessly inside. "Hello, Bert," he said in a low voice.

Whitcomb jerked visibly, swiveled his attention to the doorway. His right hand dropped swiftly to the gun at his hip.

"It's me, Johnny Locke."

Bert came off the bench in a long leap. His face broke into a smile. "Johnny! Sure wasn't expecting you, kid!"

He gripped Locke's extended hand, drew him further into the room. "What the devil brings you here?"

"Riding through," Locke said, unable to keep a slight edge from his tone. He let his glance drop to the packets of money on the table.

Bert Whitcomb's smile faded. He released Locke's hand, fell back a step. "You with that posse?"

Locke shook his head. "Probably looking for me. Carey threw me in when I showed up in town. Figured I had something to do with that holdup and killing, since I was a friend of yours. Couldn't make up my mind what the straight of it was so I jumped Luke Ford and came to find out for myself."

Bert waited out a long minute. Then, "So now you know."

"So now I know," Locke repeated. "Wouldn't believe it when I first heard it. Made no sense."

"Nothing much makes sense anymore," Bert said with a shrug. "At least, not to me. Hasn't since we lost everything."

"Not much reason to turn outlaw. Man could have started over."

"With what? You sound like Starr!" Bert said angrily. "That's what it takes to start over," he added and pointed to the money on the table. "With that Starr and I can begin —"

"Too late for that now, Bert. Starr's dead."

Bert Whitcomb slowly turned, his features paling under their tan. "Starr is dead?"

Locke nodded. "Ran across him back there on the trail. He took a rifle bullet in his back. Died a few minutes after I found him."

Bert Whitcomb sank onto the bench. "Might have known," he said in a low, hopeless voice. "Man's luck never changes. Once it goes bad, it stays bad. Starr never wanted any of this. Said we could make it without it. Only I wouldn't listen. It was me that put that bullet into him just as sure as if I held the gun."

John Locke said nothing. It was true, each and every word of it, and now Bert Whitcomb was beginning to pay the price he must face for his headstrong wildness. Bitter words had gathered on Locke's lips; scathing words of denouncement and blame and accusation. But he withheld them. There was little point in twisting the knife in the wound.

"Starr — did he give you any word for me?"

Locke said, "He wants you to give this up, Bert. Wants you to ride in with me, hand the money over to Hazen Carey and turn yourself in. You go on through with this now and it will be too late for all time."

Bert shook his head. "Already too late, Johnny."

"Maybe not. Turning yourself and the money in will work in your favor."

"You think so?"

"It's bound to. And Starr said you had

76

nothing to do with the shooting, with the killing of the guard and the driver. I'm no lawyer so I don't know how that would stack up in court but it seems to me that it would make a difference."

"Killing? Were the driver and guard killed?"

Locke said, "Yes. That money there cost the lives of three men — one of them your own brother."

In the long silence that followed Bert Whitcomb sat motionless on the rough bench. Outside, in the thick stand of trees a dove mourned plaintively. Far off to the north there was the faint, hollow sound of a gunshot.

"I don't see much use now," Bert began and stopped. "What chance would I have," he began again and once more halted, uncertain apparently of his own thoughts.

"I don't know," Locke replied. "Maybe a pretty fair chance, maybe none at all. But what chance do you have if you try to go on? Even if you manage to get by Hazen Carey and that investigator, Beahm and all that posse, there'll be somebody looking for you the rest of your life. It's something you can't beat, Bert. You just can't win!

"Starr wanted you to give it up. He figured you still had a good chance. He's dead, Bert

— mostly because of you. Best way you can make it up to him is to listen to what he wants and then go do it. Whether you want to admit it or not, he was right. He always was. I remember that."

Those were harsh, cruel words. John Locke realized that, but the moments called for extreme measures. He firmly believed Starr had been correct in thinking matters would go easier for Bert if he willingly turned himself over to the law. He would have to face the consequences, of course, but he was likely to get no more than a prison term, once all the facts were known. However, he must act quickly. The important thing was to do it all voluntarily, not wait to be arrested by Hazen Carey or by Beahm. The fact that he surrendered would weigh heavily in his favor.

He said, gently, "I'll ride in with you, Bert. And I'll stand by you. It's the only wise thing to do. But we'll have to move fast. Carey and his bunch probably aren't far off."

"I know — I guess —"

There was a slight sound behind John Locke. At the doorway. A thought raced through him. They were already too late! They had delayed too long! He started to turn. A harsh voice stalled him.

"Raise your hands, cowboy! Up high. You ain't goin' no place."

A second voice added "Reckon you'd better be doin' the same, Bert. Sounded to me like you was about to change your way of thinkin'."

John Locke lifted his hands slowly. He saw Bert's expression change swiftly as he rose to his feet. He did not raise his arms but he was careful to keep his hand well away from the pistol at his hip.

"What the hell you mean by that, Nate?" he demanded in a hard voice.

"Get that jasper's gun, Chino," Nate continued, ignoring Whitcomb. "Throw it out there into the brush."

Locke felt a hand at his side, then heard a faint thud when the pistol struck the earth somewhere in front of the shack.

"Turn around. Back up against that there wall."

Locke did as he was directed. Bert yet stood near the table, not moving. Color had returned to his face and his eyes had pulled down to narrow, angry slits. Locke had a good look at the two outlaws then. The one called Chino was short and squat with dark, sunburned skin. Black, glossy hair covered his bare arms and thrust out above the

79

throat of his shirt, climbing well up onto his neck. His eyes were small bits of glittering jet, set wide apart and deep.

The other man was slight of build with nondescript brown hair and pale, lifeless eyes. He had an empty face and his mouth was little more than a long, gray slash dividing his features. He wore his gun low, tied down and well forward. He would be Nate Corrigan.

"Don't go making any mistake about who's running this outfit," Bert said then, his voice carrying a strong measure of threat.

"I'm not," Corrigan replied softly. "I'm just bein' sure it's bein' run. That right, Chino?"

Gregg shrugged. "Sounded to us like you was fixin' to change things some, Bert. And after we went to all that hard work!"

Corrigan's glass-hard eyes drilled into Locke. "Who's this bird?"

"Once a friend of mine," Whitcomb said in an easy, off hand way. "Was just riding through on his way north."

"What was that talk he was givin' you about goin' along with him!"

"Just talk," Bert replied, brushing off the question.

"Where's Starr?" Gregg asked then, as if

suddenly remembering.

Bert slid a hasty glance at Locke. "He'll be along pretty soon," he said and let it drop there.

Corrigan came back to his original topic. "What was that this jasper was sayin' — about turnin' in the money?"

Bert laughed. "Locke here was trying to turn me pure again. Wanted me to hand it all over to the marshal."

There was a long pause. Chino Gregg finally said, "That what you figure to do?"

"Hell, no! What do you take me for?"

Locke stared at Bert Whitcomb. His words had not had any effect at all on him! He had listened, pretended to agree in part while all the time he intended to keep the stolen money. The death of Starr meant little to him, as did friendship. It appeared now that he had stalled along with Locke, kept him occupied until his two outlaw friends arrived.

Corrigan was not fully convinced. He watched Bert with steady, unblinking eyes. "Ain't the way it sounded to me," he said.

Whitcomb moved his shoulders in a gesture of resignation. "You got a thick head, Nate. Nothing ever soaks in. I was just talking to him, keeping him busy. I knew you two were out there and due to show up. And

81

I know Locke, here, and the way he handles a gun. You just be glad I had him looking this way when you came in. Otherwise one of you, maybe both, would be dead right now."

A faint interest broke across Nate Corrigan's face. "Fast, eh?"

"Too fast for me to argue with," Bert replied. "Or you either."

Whitcomb suddenly swung his glance to Locke. "No use you hanging around, Johnny. I'm satisfied the way things are. Get your horse and ride on."

"Hold up!" Corrigan broke in. "That jasper ain't goin' nowhere. This whole country is crawlin' with badge toters and trigger-happy posse riders. We turn him loose he'll go straight to them and next thing we know, we'll have them all right here in our laps."

Bert said, "Nope, not likely. He don't cotton to the law any more than we do." He stopped, turned to Locke. "You give me your word you'll ride out and keep your mouth shut, Johnny, and we'll let it go at that."

Locke started to frame a reply but Nate Corrigan cut him off. "Word or no word, that ain't enough for me! I figure to get out of this country alive so's I can spend my share of that money and I ain't riskin' it on the word of some drifter!"

Chino Gregg said, "Them's my sentiments, too. We're in this too deep now to lose out. I say we better shut this bird up for good. Otherwise we got somebody out runnin' around that can point a finger at us any time he takes the notion."

"And we better get at it, too," Corrigan added. "That posse is workin' this way. Reckon we can be expectin' them pretty soon."

He swung his cold gaze at Locke. The tall rider felt a chill travel along his spine, but his nerves were steady. He was looking death in the eye, in that moment, he knew.

"I know this man," Bert said. "Fact is, I grew up with him. Me and Starr both. We were like three brothers. He gives me his word he won't talk, I'll guarantee you that's the way it will be."

Corrigan said, "No deal, Bert. We don't leave no gates open behind us."

"You don't want to take care of him, I'll do it," Gregg offered. "Him bein' a friend of your'n and all that."

Bert Whitcomb thought for a long minute. He shrugged. "Well, could be you're right. Reckon we shouldn't take any chances. Hell of a lot of money at stake."

"Good," Corrigan said softly, his face lighting with a sort of wicked anticipation. "Want me to take care of him? Wouldn't mind findin' out just how fast he is with a gun."

Bert reached down, lifted his pistol upwards in its holster, let it drop back into place. "No, reckon it's a job for me. My fault he walked in on us. Guess it's up to me to get him out of the way now."

Whitcomb's voice was cold, his words matter of fact. Locke felt the chill move through him again. Here was a Bert Whitcomb he could never have imagined existed.

"Need some help?"

Bert said, "No. Like Nate said we better be getting out of here, Chino. You two finish putting that money into the saddlebags. We don't want no Dangerfield stage line money sacks on us. And Chino, there's a spring about a dozen steps back of the cabin. Better fill the canteens. We're liable to need water where we go. Hurry it up. This won't take me long."

He drew his pistol, leveled it at Locke. Chino Gregg wheeled to the doorway and walked outside to get the supply of water. Corrigan fell to working at the money.

"Let's go," Bert said and ducked his head toward the opening. "Keep your hands on top of your head."

"Where you takin' him?" Corrigan asked.

"Little wash about fifty yards off to the west side. Figure there's no use leaving him here for the marshal to find."

Corrigan muttered his agreement and continued at his task.

Bert said, "Sorry about this, Johnny, but you can see how it is. I got no choice. Was I in this alone it might be different but my partners don't know you like I do."

Locke, some of the disbelief now worn off, shook his head. "Never figured you'd turn out this way, Bert. An outlaw — a killer, the worst I've come across. Sure hard to believe."

"Man lives and learns," Whitcomb said absently.

They passed by Gregg, on out into the clearing and moved into the trees. At each step John Locke felt his blood run colder while the prickling along his neck and scalp increased. He looked about, seeking some avenue of escape; he searched his brain for some plan, however desperate.

He said, "Bert, this will hang you for sure. You might manage to get out of the other trouble with only a time in jail but this will be different. Several people knew I was going to see you, Sally for one. When they find me they'll figure exactly what happened."

"Keep walking," Whitcomb replied in a harsh, loud voice. "No use bawling about it, Johnny. Time comes for a man to die, best thing he can do is meet it standing up."

They reached the edge of the ravine, a narrow gash three or four feet in depth. Locke halted. The surrounding forest was stone quiet as if all living things had paused to watch the coming moments. Locke glanced to the sky, blue overhead with a threat of rain piling up in the west.

The clack of Bert's gun coming to a full cock was a monstrous sound in the tense hush. Locke steeled himself for the impact of the bullet. He would ask nothing more of Bert Whitcomb; he could not beg. He had made his own position clear, had tried to help but it had all backfired. Now there was nothing else left to be said.

"This is going to be in my back, Bert?"

The thunderous explosion of the gun was his reply. He felt no shock. He started to turn, to see what had happened. From out of nowhere something descended upon him, struck him across the head with tremendous force. The world wheeled in a circle of flashing lights and then plunged into blackness.

8

He came back to consciousness slowly, painfully. He was lying face down in the shallow arroyo. When he fell, he had pinned his left arm beneath his body. It ached now in steady accompaniment to his throbbing head.

He sat up, still slightly dazed, and looked about carefully. He was alone. He had no way of knowing how long he had been out, possibly no more than a few minutes as the sun was still well above the western horizon. He felt of his head, gingerly, where Bert Whitcomb had struck him. The spot was tender and wet. The barrel of Bert's gun, if that was what was used as a club, had broken the scalp and drawn blood.

He shook his head, clearing it of the last shadows and got unsteadily to his feet. A quick wave of dizziness swept through him but it passed quickly. He picked up his hat and climbed out of the arroyo, again cautious and wary. It was entirely possible Bert and the two outlaws were still in the shack.

A moment later he doubted the likelihood. At the edge of the ravine he found the hoof prints of three horses, drawn up in a line. Evidently Chino Gregg and Nate Corrigan, with Bert, had ridden up to have their look and assure themselves Bert had fulfilled his duty. He must have been out completely at the time, he guessed. He had apparently passed for a dead man.

He thought then of Bert Whitcomb, sought to clarify the man's intentions in his own mind. He had believed that, before Gregg and Corrigan had showed up at the cabin, Bert was on the verge of accepting his dying brother's request. Then, when the two outlaws had faced him, he had changed his thinking.

But had that been because he feared for the life of Locke? Had he just pretended to go along with the two hard cases, had faked the killing of Locke, in order to save him from certain death at the hands of Corrigan or Gregg? If so, did he still plan to return the money and give himself up when the opportunity presented itself?

It seemed so to John Locke yet he was not entirely convinced of it. That Bert had deliberately set about to save him from being murdered was apparent. Even Bert Whitcomb, changed as he was by the grinding years, thought enough of his boyhood friend to not permit such a deed. But when it came to returning the stolen money and giving himself up to the law, in accordance with Starr's wishes, Locke was not so certain.

One thing suddenly became clear to John Locke. If Bert had been stalling and did intend to give up at the first opportunity, he would need help. Chino Gregg and the flat-eyed gunman, Nate Corrigan, would not willingly agree to any such arrangement, that was sure. Bert would need some backing, and soon. Of course, it was only a guess, Locke realized, but he could take no chance on it. He would have to find Bert, help him if he did want to clear up matters.

He moved away from the arroyo, headed for the clearing and the shack. He walked fast. He had little time to spare. It soon would be dark and trailing Bert and the outlaws would be almost impossible — and delay could cost Bert Whitcomb his life.

He remembered then he was unarmed, that his gun had been taken from him and tossed into the brush. It would be lying somewhere in front of the cabin, in a direct line with the door. He altered his course and skirted the clearing, coming in at a point in front of the structure. He found the pistol almost immediately. He picked it up, examined it. It was undamaged, except for some soft earth wedged into the end of the barrel. He removed that, brushed off the weapon, tried its action and satisfied, thrust it into his holster.

He circled about to where he had picketed the bay. The horse was still there, grazing contentedly on the short, sweet grass that grew thick in the forest. He swung to the saddle and rode back to the cabin. It occurred to him that it would be a good idea to check the room over carefully. Bert would guess he would return there, once he regained consciousness, and if Bert hoped he would follow and give him aid, he would leave some sort of sign or clue as to which direction he and the outlaws would be taking.

He tied the bay in front of the shack and went first to where Bert had anchored his own mount. He examined the area immediate to that but found nothing of interest. He then looked about until he located the spot where Gregg and Corrigan had tethered their horses but neither that point nor the soft loam surrounding the spring where Gregg had filled the canteens offered any information. He returned at once to the shack.

The small canvas bags, blackly imprinted with the name of the stage company, lay on the table. He poked about through them, again found nothing. He checked the floor, scanning the marks in the accumulated dust, to no avail. There were only the prints of men's boots and the tracks of small animals, pack rats, field mice and the like.

The walls offered nothing, nor did the scummed surface of the window pane which would have been an ideal medium for conveying a message. Finally having exhausted all possibilities, he stood in the center of the room and tried to recall the things that had been said, the words that had passed between Bert and the outlaws while he had waited for them to decide his fate.

There had been nothing, so far as he could remember, that would indicate their intended destination. He was sure of that. The talk had been mostly concerning himself — and the two men's half suspicions of Bert. He could recall not the slightest hint of even the direction they planned to follow, much less any specific clue as to a town they would head for.

Impatient with himself, with his failure to

come up with anything of value, Locke tried to put himself in Bert's position. Which way would he go if he were in his boots? Not south for in that direction lay the town of Three Forks and to ride that way would mean to ride straight into trouble. West, then, over the mountains? Hardly. It was many days of slow, rough going to the first far settlement and he knew they had not been prepared for such a difficult trip.

To the north, not likely either. While brushy and thickly covered with trees, the country was fairly overrun by Marshal Hazen Carey and his posse. Heading out in that direction would be courting disaster. East. It had to be east. The hills extended for several miles before they flattened out into long plains. Cover, while not so plentiful as that to the north, was ample. Three men moving with care could escape and reach the wild, rugged brakes country. And Bert Whitcomb well knew that area; a wide land lying in a huge wash, piled in vast disorder and confusion with huge rocks, thorny brush, scrub trees and glittering sand. A waterless waste, it extended eastward mile upon mile, a desolate world few men ever crossed and none sought to follow out in length. It all added up swiftly then for John Locke. It accounted for the canteens Bert had insisted upon. They had headed for the brakes.

Locke wheeled about. He crossed the breadth of the cabin, stepped through the doorway into the open — and froze. A sharp voice reached out from the thick brush only steps away, nailing him to where he stood.

"All right, Locke, haul up! There's a half a dozen guns covering you!"

It was the marshal, Hazen Carey.

Locke, angered by his own carelessness, lifted his arms slowly, watched the lawman emerge from the thick shrubbery. Others materialized: Beahm, the Dangerfield investigator, Deputy Luke Ford, Tilton, Morgan and several other posse members.

"Two, three you men stay outside. Keep in the bushes, just in case somebody else shows up. Get those horses out of sight."

A man interrupted the marshal. "What about that bay of his'n?"

Before the old lawman could answer, Beahm laughed in that unpleasant way of his and said, "Leave him there. Maybe he'll be the honey that'll draw the rest of the flies."

The man who asked the question ignored Beahm, waited for Carey to make his reply. Carey said, "Leave him be where he is." He turned back to Locke.

"Get his gun, Luke."

The deputy moved up beside Locke, careful not to place himself between the tall rider and the guns that covered him. He had a large, bluish swelling beneath his left eye and a place on his chin where the skin had been scraped away. His eyes glowed brightly as he watched Locke, revealing the hatred that now lay within him. Locke, watching him closely, wondered how long he had remained in the cell of the jail before being discovered and released.

"And this time see if you can hang on to it," Hazen Carey said with cutting sarcasm.

Ford thrust Locke's gun into his waistband, glared steadily at his one-time prisoner. "Don't fret none about it, marshal. This jasper ever fools me again, it'll be somebody else's fault, not mine!"

"Things that happen to you are always somebody else's fault," the lawman murmured. He swung his attention back to Locke. "Inside. Keep your hands over your head."

Locke retreated into the shack. Carey, Beahm and Luke Ford pressed in behind him. Two more members of the posse took up posts at the doorway.

In the tight hush that had fallen over the

small room, Matt Beahm said, "Well, marshal, looks like you were right about this fiddle-footed ridgerunner after all."

Carey removed his hat, brushed wearily at his thick, snowy hair. It had been a long, hard day for the old lawman and it laid its mark across his craggy features in sagging lines of fatigue. He shook his head.

"Maybe," he answered. He squinted at Locke. "That right, son? I have you figured?"

Locke returned the lawman's glance. "Meaning?"

"That you were in on this holdup and killing with your foster brothers and somebody else?"

Locke shook his head. "Still wrong, marshal."

"Adds up," Carey stated. "You broke jail then run straight here. Looks like they was supposed to meet you in this shack. Only they didn't wait for you."

"Looks like everybody was too late," Beahm said and moved to the table. He picked up several of the canvas money sacks, waved them at Carey. "They've been here and gone, sure enough."

Carey took one of the bags, examined it critically. "No doubt." He lifted his sharp eyes to Locke. "Anything you'd like to say about it?"

Locke thought quickly. He could tell them they were right, or partly so. That Bert and the two outlaws were only a few minutes away, most likely heading east and thus take a long step in clearing himself of any complicity. But in so doing he would also ruin any hopes Bert had of turning himself and the money in and trying to start a new life. It could virtually amount to signing Bert's death warrant for he know that Bert, if cornered and feeling it was too late then to make any amends, would elect to fight it out.

Locke shrugged. "You're doing all the figuring, marshal."

Carey stared at him thoughtfully, tugged at the trailing ends of his mustache. "Might help things for you, son, was you to talk up and give us a hand."

A curse suddenly ripped from Matt Beahm's lips. He stepped forward, anger flushing his broad face. He swung a huge, hamlike fist. It caught Locke in the belly, taking him unaware. Locke slammed back against the wall from the impact of the blow. Breath gushed from his mouth and behind him the window rattled loudly. Half-doubled from pain, he did not see the second blow coming. It caught him on the side of the face, snapped his head up. Beahm drove on in mercilessly. He followed with a left that skidded off the tall rider's forehead.

A wild fury ripped through John Locke. He was faintly aware of Hazen Carey's yells at the investigator but he paid no attention to the aroused lawman. He brought a hard right hand up from his heels, pistoned it into Beahm's midsection. He crossed swiftly with a left that cracked against the big man's jaw. He staggered him with a right to the head.

Beahm fell back, retreating on uncertain legs across the room. Locke was after him like a killer cat, driving relentlessly, hammering away with knotted fists that raised a dull, meaty sound when they struck. Carey was shouting at the top of his voice. Someone else was clawing at his arms, his shoulders, seeking to hold him back. Something struck him across the back of the neck, something hard. It stalled him momentarily, brought a measure of reason to his infuriated brain.

"Damnit!" Hazen Carey bellowed into his ear. "Cut out this fighting or I'll lay open your head with this gun barrel!"

Luke Ford and another man seized Locke's arms and dragged him back to the opposite side of the room, now choked with dust stirred up by the two scuffling men. Beahm sagged against the far wall, his face flushed, blood dripping from his nostrils. He was gasping for breath, his huge chest heaving with the effort.

Hazen Carey, white with anger, glared at him through fierce, old eyes. "Next time you pull a stunt like that, Beahm, you and your boys can mount up and ride the hell out of here! You hear me? Nobody's going to maul a prisoner of mine around without cause!"

"Cause!" Beahm yelled in a strangled voice. "What more cause do you want? He knows exactly where the rest of his bunch has gone with that money! He could take us right to them! You let me and my boys have him for a few minutes and I'll fair make him talk up!"

Carey favored the investigator with a scornful smile. "You sure your two men would be enough? Maybe you ought to take the whole blasted posse!"

"I could do better with it!" Beahm shot back, hotly. "Day's about gone and we're no place."

"Maybe you ought to scare up a posse of your own," Hazen Carey said icily. "Seeing as how you don't like the way I run mine."

"Could be a good idea," Beahm replied,

rubbing at his jaw.

The lawman turned about, placed his back to the investigator. He faced Locke. "Where's the rest of your bunch? Now's the time to speak up."

"Not my bunch," Locke answered.

Carey shook his head. "You already proved that is a lie when you broke jail and rode straight here. If you hadn't been one of them you wouldn't have done that."

"Could be other reasons."

"Don't see what they could be."

"I figured the Whitcombs most likely were innocent. I wanted to warn them you were coming for them."

"Why? You think they got good reason to be afraid of the law?"

"Not the law," Locke said slowly, "but of a lynch mob. That's the way it was bound to end up."

Hazen Carey's eyes flashed. "No lynch mob ever took a man away from me yet!"

Locke said, "First time for everything."

A man rode into the clearing, dismounted. He walked to the doorway of the cabin and said, "Marshal?"

Carey stepped to his side, leaned forward while the rider whispered something to him. The lawman nodded and returned to his position in the center of the room.

"Moment ago," he began after a short pause, "you told me you figured the Whitcombs were innocent. Don't you think so now?"

Locke shrugged. "Man's got a right to his opinion, marshal. I'm not saying mine's changed or not."

"Maybe it'll help you make up your mind if I tell you Starr Whitcomb is dead. They found him a couple hours ago, tied across his own saddle. Horse was about halfway between here and town."

Beahm stepped forward, his face suddenly alive. "I guess that proves it all out now, marshal! It's the Whitcombs we want for sure. That driver said one of the outlaws was shot."

Carey ignored the investigator. He kept his attention placed upon Locke. "What about it? You still say the Whitcomb boys had nothing to do with it?"

"Maybe he even knows all about Starr being dead," Luke Ford suggested. "Could be he was there when they slung him across his saddle."

Locke was guarding his tongue, being extremely careful of his answers. He had managed to maintain a shadow of doubt in their minds, where the Whitcombs were concerned, up to this point. The finding of

Starr's dead body now ended that. But there still was the hope that Bert would turn himself in, would do as Starr wished. Therefore, all he could do was to continue to play out the hand. The less he appeared to know about anything, the better all around, he concluded.

Beahm faced Locke, a triumphant look on his face. "Reckon that sort of proves where you stand, cowboy. Makes all that jawin' you been giving us a lot of hogwash!" He swung abruptly to Carey. "Marshal, to my way of thinking, he's as guilty as the others. He's one of them and he knows right where they can be found. The quicker we make him talk, the sooner we'll have them all behind bars."

"Get a rope, somebody!" a voice just outside the doorway shouted.

"Forget it!" Hazen Carey barked instantly. "Be nothing like that around here. Anyway," he added, looking at Locke closely, "I'm not so sure he's lying. He could have come up here to warn them. That would account for him being at this shack. He'd been one of them, why didn't he ride on, too?"

"Just forgetting that he was late and they went on without waiting for him. It was probably because he had to take care of the one that got shot, Starr or whatever his

101

name is," Beahm said. "I'd give you odds that he was the one who loaded him on that horse and started it for town."

Carey glanced at Locke. "You got any answer to that?"

John Locke shook his head.

Beahm went on. "He probably set it up with the other two to take the money, including his share, and ride on. He'll meet them later somewheres. Or maybe they already split up the cash, seeing as how they've taken it out of the bags. I tell you, marshal, he could give us all the answers if you'd let me make him talk."

"Maybe," Hazen Carey murmured. "And maybe not. He don't look to me much like the kind you can make do anything, unless he was willing."

Locke hid a smile at the old lawman's words. He said, "Obliged, marshal. Reckon you're right. But I'll tell you this much. I'm not mixed up in it and I sure don't know where they went."

"You had any idea, would you tell it?" Beahm demanded.

Locke met the investigator's hostile gaze. "No point in answering that," he said coolly, "since I've already said I don't know where they headed for."

"Just like I figured," Beahm said and

whirled about in disgust. "All right then, marshal, if you don't figure to make him talk, let's get started after the rest of them. Going to be dark in a couple of hours. We wait much longer they'll be clean out of the Territory!"

"Day's about gone, sure enough," Carey said mildly. "We'll quit then. Can't expect these men to keep looking after they can't see."

Beahm halted in his tracks. "You mean you're calling off the posse at dark?" he asked in an exasperated voice.

"Be like looking for a buckshot in a sack of beans," the lawman said. "And too hard on men and horses."

"But you can't quit!" the investigator cried. "We're this close, you can't pull out now! That'd be like just turning them loose. By damn, me and my boys ain't going to do it!"

Carey said, "Sounds like you and your boys just formed your own posse," and turned to his deputy, Ford. "Luke, pick yourself a man and the pair of you take Locke here back to town. Jail him and this time be dang sure he stays jailed."

Ford's expression was dour. "This time he'll stay," he said. "He won't get out again."

"Better put your manacles on him. That,

maybe, will slow him down if he gets any smart ideas."

Ford reached for his back pocket, looked startled for a moment and then nodded. "Sure enough, marshal. Don't you worry none about him."

"I won't," Carey said curtly. "But if he gets away, you better do some worrying!"

The deputy nodded his head at one of the posse members, standing just inside the doorway. "You, there, Snyder. Give me a hand."

Snyder, a young, husky cowboy stepped deeper into the room. He drew his gun. "Sure, Luke."

"Outside," Ford nudged Locke. "And climb up on that horse of yours, easy and slow like."

9

Locke crossed the room, passed through the doorway and walked into the clearing. Behind him he heard Marshal Hazen Carey summoning his men, ordering them to mount up. He reached his bay horse, stepped to the saddle, keeping his movements deliberate and natural. Luke Ford was only steps behind him, covering him with a cocked pistol. He knew the deputy needed only the slightest of excuses to shoot.

A full dozen riders were suddenly in the clearing, awaiting orders. The delay he had caused them should have given Bert time to be well on his way, afforded him the chance to escape from Chino Gregg and Nate Corrigan — if that was what he really planned to do.

"All right, Beahm," he heard Hazen Carey say. "You and your men still with this posse or you taking off with one of your own?"

And Beahm's answer: "We'll ride with you, marshal. Leastwise, for a spell."

"Then it's my orders you'll be following."

The posse rode out of the clearing, into the concealing band of trees and brush. Locke glanced to Ford. He wondered why the deputy had not placed the manacles about his wrists, as Carey had directed him to do. He recalled the startled look on Ford's tough face, one almost of shock. He remembered then the encounter earlier that day in the jail, and understood the reason. He had used the deputy's own handcuffs to bind his wrists together when he made an escape. Ford had evidently neglected to bring them along after he had managed to get free. And he did not want Hazen Carey to know of his carelessness.

Snyder came up, drew his gun and took a position before him. Ford walked quietly off into the brush, to return a moment later on his horse.

"Let's ride," he said. "You lead out, Locke. We'll be right behind you."

"Ain't you goin' to put your handcuffs on him, like the marshal said?" Snyder asked.

Ford threw a hasty glance in the direction Carey had taken. The lawman was no longer to be seen. "Won't need to," he said then, settling into his saddle. "We'll be settin' on his tail all the way and we'll have two guns pointin' at his backbone. He makes a move to break, he's dead."

"I don't know," Snyder mumbled. "The marshal said —"

"Forget it!" Ford snapped.

Locke half turned, glanced back at the deputy. He grinned.

Ford's eyes sparkled angrily. He gestured impatiently with his pistol. "Move out!" he said.

They rode from the clearing, Locke in the lead on his bay, Snyder and Luke Ford flanking him, and a length behind. The two men had their weapons drawn and ready and their nerves — Ford's at least — were honed to a thin edge. Escaping from them would be difficult and certainly most dangerous.

But escape he must if he were to help Bert Whitcomb. There were only two, possibly three hours of daylight remaining but in that time Hazen Carey, Beahm and the posse, having now a starting point, could fan out, form an effective forage line and efficiently search the country for Bert and the two outlaws.

Although Bert and the pair would now have an ample start they would be unaware that Carey had withdrawn the posse for a time and gathered at the shack. They would believe the men searching for them were yet scattered about in the forest and canyons and they would proceed with caution and slow pace. Their lead would melt quickly away once Carey and his riders began to move. It was doubtful that darkness would fall soon enough to give them sanctuary.

He slid a glance over his shoulder. Ford had returned his gun to its holster and was presently occupied in rolling himself a cigarette. Snyder, however, was keeping a close watch, his gaze level and suspicious.

"Gettin' ideas?" Ford asked in a low, silky tone. "Figurin' up how you might make a try for it?"

Locke made no reply. He let his glance return to the path ahead. It was wide in this particular section of the forest, with brush scanty and trees spaced well apart.

"Just you go right ahead," the deputy invited. "Make your play. Suit me just fine. I figure I owe you somethin' for the way you jumped me back there in jail. Don't know any better way to square up than have you try to escape."

John Locke was only half listening. He was thinking, reaching back into his memory, trying to recall the land through which they were passing. He had spent most of his life there, had ridden through this particular section numberless times; now he was endeavoring to remember each foot of the trail and the nature of the country lying beside it.

They would continue on in a fairly straight manner for some distance, it seemed to him. Then the trail would drop off the low ridge it now followed, would wind down into a narrow ravine. It would pass along the floor of the gash, heading in a more or less direct line for the main road to Three Forks. Once there, they would be in broad, open country and his chance for escape would end. If he were to make his try, it would have to come soon, before they broke out of the trees and scrubby oak and choppy ravines.

It came sooner than he expected. They reached the end of the ridge. The trail swung abruptly to the left, started down into the wash, as Locke had remembered. It was an easy, gradual slant. He cut the bay off the ridge, aware that Ford and Snyder had been compelled to drop into single file. Snyder was directly behind him while the deputy brought up the rear.

Locke was halfway down. Quite suddenly Snyder's horse stumbled or perhaps shied at something along the edge of the trail. He veered to one side, then lunged forward.

His long head snapped upward as he sought
to avoid the rump of Locke's bay. Snyder
yelled as his mount pivoted awkwardly, went
to his knees and blocked the trail in a frantic
effort to keep from going down completely.

John Locke, alert for any such moment,
seized the opportunity. He drove spurs into
the bay, headed him down the remainder of
the path in a reckless plunge. Behind him
Ford shouted a curse. A pistol cracked
sharply but Locke did not hear the singing
of a bullet and judged it to be far wide. He
could hear Snyder fighting with his horse
and Ford's swearing was a steady, blistering
racket.

He reached the bottom of the slope just
as the pound of Ford's pursuit reached him.
He swung sharply left, ducking into a thick,
unbroken stand of oak. It was slow going
but he was well concealed and that was
what he needed most in that moment. He
must stay out of the deputy's sight.

"Cut over to the right!"

Luke Ford's shout to Snyder told him the
cowboy had recovered and was back in the
chase.

"We got to hem him in! He's somewhere
down in that brush. Don't let him get past
you!"

Locke, bent low over the bay, took a long

breath. It was going to be close and if Ford could draw near enough, he would open up with his gun. He reached down, patted the straining bay's neck. It was rough, hard going. The brush was dense, resisted their forward movement on every side. Time after time the bay was forced to crash his way through the leafy barriers.

He was making far too much noise to shake Ford and Snyder off his trail, he realized. But it was impossible to slow down, to try and travel more quietly. Ford was only a short distance behind him while Snyder rode off to the right, also very near. He would have to do something soon. That was becoming apparent, too. The bay could not keep up such a grueling pace for long. Bucking through the brush was a little like trying to run a horse through deep snow.

He glanced ahead. They were doubling back toward the mountains. He could see the band of shrubbery through which they raced was thinning out, would soon dissolve into rocks and scattered trees which marked the area along the foot of the higher hills. He looked back over his shoulder. Ford was not in view but was still coming on. The sounds of his approach were loud and clear.

Without hesitation Locke cut the bay to the right. It would be suicide to break out into the open ahead of Luke Ford. He would feel a half a dozen bullets in his back before he could cover ten feet. Better to take his chances with the cowboy, Snyder. He found a narrow lane, which ran at a right angle to the course he had been traveling. The bay, grateful for the change, stretched out his long legs in a hard run.

They pounded across in front of Snyder, giving that man only a fleeting glimpse. He immediately hauled up, sent a shout into the quiet of the forest. Locke could no longer hear Ford but was not sure if it was because of the distance between them or that the deputy, realizing his escaping prisoner was no longer ahead of him, had pulled to a stop.

"Over here! Over here!"

Snyder's strident summons echoed through the trees. "He's headin' for town!"

Such had not been noted by Locke. The bay, reluctant to leave the open lane had thundered on without slackening, following down a passageway that curved gently toward the south. It came to an end a short quarter mile later. They plunged into a thin stand of tamarack. Locke allowed the bay to run on, churning up dust across the dry ground when he left the lane behind. Then, well hidden by another stand of heavier growth, he swung hard left and pulled to a halt.

There, behind an effective screen of oak, he waited and watched. Snyder broke into view first, riding his little horse at top speed down the passageway between the trees. His head came up when he saw the dust beyond the tamarack.

"Snyder!" Luke Ford's questioning shout rolled down from the far end of the lane.

"Here! He's still headin' south, for town!"

Locke watched Ford thunder by in pursuit of the cowboy, heard the cowboy race after the man he thought was beyond the dust cloud. He brushed the sweat from his forehead, grinned. That had been too close. He wheeled the bay about, pointed him eastward toward the brakes. Next job was to get there ahead of the posse. He had to find Bert and give him some help before it was too late. But there was one serious drawback.

He had no weapon.

10

He should quit now.

He should pull up stakes and get the hell out of the country. Common sense told him it was the smart thing to do. Starr was dead. Bert was guilty and, to all intents and purposes, beyond help. He ought to forget about him for it was a matter of law now. And he just as well ought to forget Sally Dean, too. Chances are he was only fooling himself where she was concerned.

To delay longer might cost him his future with the Walking W outfit in Wyoming — and it could even cost him his life out there in the night if Beahm and his two men slipped up on him, unnoticed. The smart thing for him to do was get out while he still had a chance.

But, somehow, that idea, with all its undeniable logic, did not sit well with John Locke. There was his promise to Starr Whitcomb, the obligation he felt to the family itself. Perhaps his foster brother was beyond any large measure of help now but there might be something he could do; and if he planned to give himself up to Hazen Carey, he would need help in doing so. Beahm and Tilton and Morgan would probably shoot on sight; they would never permit him to reach the marshal alive, which was an odd attitude for a person such as Beahm to take. But Locke had heard it from the investigator's own lips.

Then, there was the very real possibility of a lynch mob taking Bert out and hanging him, once he was in the hands of Hazen Carey. The marshal would need help in preventing that. And before anything could be done, Bert would have to get away from Nate Corrigan and Chino Gregg. There, possibly, lay the greatest danger, for the two gunmen would not relinquish their claims willingly. They would never agree to any such about face on the part of Bert and gunplay was bound to result. Here again, Bert would need him.

Further, there was Sally Dean. Just what he hoped to learn or prove where she was concerned, was not entirely clear in his mind. The discovery that she and Bert had not married had thrown him off balance and talking to her about it had only confused him more. Several times he had found himself wondering if she still loved Bert or now was only interested in his welfare, as a once close friend, and fearful of the consequences he must eventually face. Starr had spoken lightly of the affair, even intimated his brother had never really been serious about Sally, only professed to be so because of John Locke.

That was difficult to believe. He could not believe Bert Whitcomb harbored any such ill feeling for him, yet Starr had said it was so and Starr Whitcomb was not a man to lie. Locke stirred restlessly in his saddle, disturbed greatly by such a thought. Perhaps Starr had gotten it all wrong, had misinterpreted things somehow. Quite suddenly it became clear to John Locke that the answer to it all lay with Bert; his surrendering to Hazen Carey would cancel Locke's obligation to the family and — would clarify Sally Dean's feelings for Bert and for himself.

He had no choice but to continue. He moved the bay out at a slow walk, going quietly and with care. He had abandoned any thoughts of taking a long, roundabout route to the brakes but kept instead to a straight and direct line. Mathew Beahm and his riders, as well as any other posse members who had chosen to stay with them, could be anywhere in the widely flung forest and hills. It would be senseless and a waste of time to intentionally try and avoid them.

The best course was to simply cut across the country, keep a sharp watch for any riders. Just trying to guess their positions in advance would be a little like trying to read the mind of the wind.

It was a full night with starlight and the moon filtering down in a silver filigree through the trees. It was not difficult to travel although the bay was beginning to show signs of wear. Locke held him to an easy pace, however, conserving his strength and hoping it would not become necessary for him to make another hard, fast run.

Far back on the slopes of the Blackfoot hills a coyote set up a cry and several times in their hushed passage they startled night birds and small animals from the brush surrounding them. A faint breeze sprang up, blowing in out of the west, an almost certain indication of rain, he recalled. An hour after that, when he paused at a small spring to rest and water the bay for a few minutes, he saw the first heavy clouds gathering overhead. Light began to fade gradually and he realized he would be lucky if he didn't get a thorough wetting before morning.

He tarried at the waterhole for a quarter hour and then pushed on into the night, now almost black under the shadow of the approaching storm. He should not be far from the brakes now, he figured. Not more than two or three miles. He hoped the rain would hold off until he reached that point. A sudden squall would obliterate any trail Bert and the two outlaws might have left in the sandy bottom of the wash.

He was nearer than he thought. A short mile later he was at the extreme edge of the forest and on the lip of the brakes country with its sprawling expanse of rock and brush and scrub growth. He crossed the narrow strip of intervening ground without waiting and rode down into the wash. He wished again the storm had held off; it was too dark to see the trail from the saddle and he was unwilling to expend the time it would require to get down and proceed on foot. He decided to ride on, to go deeper into the badlands and get a considerable distance between himself and the forest — and Matt Beahm. Then he would begin a search on foot. Were he Bert, he reasoned, he would have ridden well into the brakes before calling a halt.

He pressed on for a good half hour and

then stopped. He dismounted, tied the bay to a stout clump of mesquite and climbed to the top of a large boulder. To the east he could see only the vague, ragged formations of the brakes, the irregular horizons of rock and brush and low hills. To the south and north lay similar ground. To the west — his heart beat quickened when he swung his gaze back over the route he had just traversed — he saw the faint, sheltered flickerings of a small camp fire.

His first thought was that it was Mathew Beahm and his two riders. But that did not sound reasonable. They could hardly have been that far ahead of him, or that far to the east, either. It had to be Bert Whitcomb and the outlaws, Gregg and Corrigan. He had overridden their camp in the darkness, set up, most likely, in some cave or similar formation.

He moved back to the bay quickly, swung onto the saddle. He turned the weary horse about and within ten yards promptly lost sight of the fire's glow. But he had marked it well in his mind and continued on. It came into view a few minutes later and, taking precautions, he again left the saddle and walked ahead of his horse. Mounted he would be considerably higher than the surrounding vegetation and might become easily visible, silhouetted against the sky.

It was Bert and the outlaws. They had made their camp in a small hollow around which rocks and brush formed a natural wall on three sides. It was easy to see now how he had gone by them, not over a hundred yards to the south, and not realized they were there.

He tethered the bay in a sheltering clump of tamarack and approached the camp on hands and knees. Without a weapon he would have to depend upon surprise and trust that Bert would react swiftly and correctly to overcome Gregg and Nate Corrigan. He reached the lip of the small bowl, removed his hat and worked his way to its edge. The three men sat around the fire, smoking. Chino Gregg had a bottle, almost empty, in his hand. The saddlebags into which Locke had earlier seen Bert placing the stolen money, lay on the ground between them.

"Time for it is now," Gregg said, tossing the butt of his cigarette into the flames. In the hushed, threatening quiet, his voice carried well. "That way, if we get split up, we'll each have our share."

"Sure," Corrigan agreed. "You can hold your brother's part. He might not show up until daylight, maybe later than that. Me,

I'd like to get out of this country fast as I can."

The two outlaws still were unaware of Starr Whitcomb's death, Locke realized. Bert, for some reason, had not told them of it.

"Which way you be heading?" Bert asked.

Corrigan swung a lazy glance at him. "It make any difference?"

"No, was just wondering. Not good for us all to go the same direction. Might as well stay together if we do that."

"Any way but south," Gregg observed dryly.

"You got some special reason for us not splittin' up that money now and pullin' out?" Corrigan asked, his tone faintly suspicious.

Locke glanced about, seeking something to hold in his hand, something that would pass momentarily in the darkness for a pistol. His fingers closed about a short length of branch. It might get by as the barrel of a gun. Bert, apparently, was stalling for time but the outlaws would not wait much longer. He would need help.

"Keep your shirt on, Nate," Bert replied easily. "Just don't want any mistakes made, that's all."

Locke believed he understood Whitcomb's

motives then. He was hoping help, in the shape of Locke, would arrive before it became necessary to give in to Gregg and Corrigan. He was putting it off to the last possible moment. Locke placed the bit of branch in his hand, holding it as he would a revolver. He rose suddenly to his feet.

"Stay put! You're covered!"

An oath burst from Chino Gregg's lips. He sat up straight, stiffened. Corrigan did not move.

"All right, Bert," Locke called. "Take their guns."

Whitcomb scrambled to his feet quickly. He reached down, pulled Gregg's weapon and then Corrigan's. He tossed them out of the hollow into the darkness beyond.

"A damned double cross!" Gregg said in a bitter, savage way.

"Keep your gun on him," Locke warned and started to move closer.

Whitcomb stepped back from the two outlaws. A tight smile was on his handsome face. He glanced at Locke, saw the stick in his hand. In the next moment the monstrous hush was shattered by the explosion of his gun. Nate Corrigan yelled and flung himself out full length, clutching at his breast.

"What the hell —" Chino Gregg yelled in alarm and leaped to his feet.

The impact of Bert's second shot bowled him over. He was dead before he struck the ground.

John Locke stood as a man transfixed. Horror flooded through him in a sickening wave. Death was no stranger to him, violent or otherwise, but he was shocked by the scene he had just witnessed. He halted at the edge of the firelight, stared at Whitcomb.

"You got here just right," Bert said in a normal, matter of fact voice. "Worked out fine."

Locke's face was a grim mask. "There was no call to kill those men. That was pure murder, Bert! Nothing but cold-blooded murder! They weren't even armed!"

"Maybe," Whitcomb said, methodically replacing the spent cartridges in his gun. "But I know that pair, kid. Tricky. And real cute. Man never be safe a minute with them around." He completed the reloading of his weapon but did not slide it back into its holster. "Come alone?"

Locke nodded. "Who you figure would be with me?"

Bert laughed. "Thought maybe you'd joined up with Hazen and his posse." He moved in nearer to the fire but maintained a distance from Locke who had also come

123

in closer. "Right sorry I had to crease your skull back there at the shack. Only thing I could do. Nate and Chino would have done you in for sure, had I let them have their way."

"Much obliged," Locke said without feeling. "We better get started for town."

Bert Whitcomb's brows lifted. "Town?"

Locke glanced at the man sharply. "You changed your mind about turning yourself and the money in to Carey?"

Whitcomb laughed again, a harsh, dry sound in the silence. "Me? Give myself and all this money up? Where'd you get that idea, kid?"

"Starr —"

"Starr was a damned fool. Reckon I'm sorry he's dead but it was bound to happen sooner or later. He just wasn't cut out for this kind of thing. Nope, I'm heading out. I got plenty of money now. I don't have to split with nobody — unless maybe you, Johnny, you'd like to throw in —"

"Forget it, Bert," Locke cut in coldly. He faced the man he thought he knew. "You never intended to do what Starr wanted, did you? You just strung me along, like a calf on a rope —"

"Let's just say I didn't want to see you get hurt because of old times' sake."

Locke said, "And now?"

"Still don't want you hurt," Whitcomb said. "There's no use of it. I'm going to walk over and get on my horse and ride out of here. That's the way it will be."

"You're not going anywhere, Bert, except back to Three Forks with me."

Whitcomb eyed him thoughtfully. "You figure to stop me with that Quaker gun in your hand?"

Locke tossed the bit of wood into the fire. "No, with my hands."

Bert shrugged. "Don't go getting any ideas like that, Johnny. You're my friend, maybe even more than that, but it won't shuck any corn if you get in my way. I'm looking out for myself and I finally got what I want; a lot of money. And I sure aim to keep it."

"Forget it. It's a fool thing to do. You get by me and ride off with that money, you'll never get a chance to stop. You'll be riding the rest of your life."

"Sounds like Starr talking," Bert said. "And you think like him, too. You can quit preaching. I'm through with this penny-ante living."

"You'd be a lot better off right this minute if you had listened to Starr. They're gunning for you and if you manage to get by that investigator and his crew, you're still apt to be caught and strung up."

"For killing them?" Bert asked and motioned to the lifeless bodies of Chino Gregg and Nate Corrigan. "Not much they wouldn't. That pair is wanted by every sheriff in the country. Most likely they'd hand me a vote of thanks for doing their dirty work for them."

"I didn't mean them," Locke said. "I'm thinking about that stage driver and the guard." Locke had reached the point where he realized talk was getting him nowhere. The only answer was to somehow get the pistol away from Bert. Then he would have the upper hand. He said, "What about Sally? You thought how this is all going to hit her?" He moved a step nearer Whitcomb.

"Lot of Sallys where I'll go. Fact, I'll find one in every town."

Locke took another step. Bert grinned at him, shook his head. "You got something up your sleeve, Johnny? You thinking about jumping me?"

Locke made no reply, merely stared at Whitcomb in a steady, unblinking manner.

"Don't make me do something I won't like, kid. I'm still going to leave."

"You'll have to kill me first," Locke said and moved once again.

Bert Whitcomb's face stiffened, went suddenly bleak and cold. "I'm not just talking to hear the noise. If I have to use this gun, Johnny, I will!"

"Then you'll sure have to," Locke murmured.

From the darkness beyond the fan of firelight, Mathew Beahm's voice suddenly laid itself across them like a long-reaching bull whip.

"Now, you boys go right ahead, kill yourselves! But first I'll take that money. Don't either of you move!"

11

Bert Whitcomb sucked in a deep breath. Locke saw him start to raise his gun, still in his hand and hanging at his side.

"Don't try it!" Beahm barked from the shadows. "Not unless you want to die."

Bert allowed his arm to relax. He looked across the dwindling fire to Locke. "Who's this?"

"Beahm. Special investigator for the stage line."

"Thought you said you were alone."

"I am. Beahm and a couple of others are working this on their own. Guess they didn't quit when the posse did."

There were faint sounds in the rocks and brush as Mathew Beahm worked in closer. He was a careful man. He remained beyond the firelight's reach, preferring to do his talking from the darkness, at least for the time.

"Drop that gun," he said to Whitcomb.

"Then step away from it."

Bert hesitated, reluctant to comply. Without a weapon he was powerless to do anything and this he apparently was realizing.

"Drop it!" Beahm snapped the order, sharply.

Whitcomb allowed the pistol to fall to the ground without further delay.

"Now get away from it!"

Bert moved off a half a dozen paces, came to a stop.

"Now, you, ridgerunner, get over there beside him. And don't either of you get the notion to grab up that gun. I'll put a bullet straight through your head, was you to try."

John Locke walked slowly into the small hollow. He skirted the fire and came to a halt an arm's length away from Whitcomb.

Bert glanced at him, grinned. "Looks like we're in the soup, Johnny. Neither of us going nowhere. That bronc peeler talks like he means business."

"You can bet on it," Locke murmured.

"Wished he'd come on out where I could have a look at him. Spooky, talking to a man in the dark like this."

"One of you," Beahm called from the night, "step over to that fire and throw some wood on it. Do it real slow and easy. Need a little more light to see by."

Locke did as he was ordered. He passed within a yard of Bert Whitcomb's pistol and he had a sudden urge to throw himself upon it, snatch it up and roll away, firing as he did so. But it would be a fool's move; even if he got his hands on the weapon, he would have no target at which to shoot. Beahm was invisible in the blackness of the night and was continually moving.

He built up the flames until the brightness flooded the hollow and reached farther out into the night.

"Fine, just fine," Beahm said. "Now, get back to where you were."

Locke resumed his position near Whitcomb. In the tense silence, broken only by the popping of dry branches in the fire, Bert drew his attention.

"We got one chance," he said in a low whisper. "We both jump him when he gets close."

"Be a fool move," Locke replied. "You can't outrun a bullet."

"Maybe, but he couldn't get us both. He knows that. And it would slow him down some, figuring which one of us to take. That's all we need, a couple of seconds."

Locke shook his head. "No reason for me to stick out my neck. You're the one in trouble. All I got to do is let him take me in, then I'll prove I've got nothing to do with that holdup." It was not exactly that simple, thought Locke, but he was hoping to keep Bert from doing something foolhardy.

"What's all the gab about?" Beahm broke in from the edge of the swale. "You two trying to cook up something? If so, take my advice and forget it. I take no chances." He stepped into the light, halted on the opposite side of the fire. He saw for the first time apparently, the bodies of Gregg and Corrigan. "Who're they?"

"Couple of old friends," Whitcomb said in a dry voice. "We had a little argument."

Beahm lifted his glance. "You're Bert Whitcomb, I take it."

Bert made no answer. He watched Beahm start to circle the fire, evidently for a better look at the two dead outlaws. To Locke he murmured, "When I yell, jump him."

Locke said, "No, thanks. I'm through with this. Washed up."

"You want to take me in, don't you?" Bert persisted. "You want me to do what Starr said. This will be your last chance."

Locke shifted his gaze to Whitcomb. He knew he could not trust the man, could put no faith in his words at all. But this mo-

131

ment could be different, could have changed everything, he told himself. Facing Beahm, as Bert was, and knowing the inevitable consequences, he could at least be realizing where his best interests lay. Possibly he was sincere. Of course it could be a little hard to explain to Marshal Hazen Carey why they had overpowered the stage lines investigator but it would not be too difficult. There was little love between the two men.

"Know that pair," Beahm said. "Run into them over in Kansas couple of years ago." He glanced at Bert. "This the rest of your bunch?"

"They were."

Beahm nodded slowly. "You and your brother, Starr, these two here and this drifter, Locke. That the bunch you hit the stage with?"

Bert said, "Locke had nothing to do with it. Just happened along."

The investigator cocked his head at Locke. "Well, looks like you were telling it straight all along. Too bad."

Locke only half heard the reply and it went unnoticed. He was thinking of Bert Whitcomb's words, of his proposal. He was wondering if he could now, finally, believe what his foster brother was saying. And if so, was it worth the risk such a reckless move would involve? Bert would need all the help he could muster, once he was brought to an accounting for his crimes, that was certain. In fact, John Locke was fairly well convinced there was little anyone could do for him now. Too many things had happened, too much blood had been spilled for the law to take a kindly attitude toward Bert Whitcomb. But if he turned himself in — the same reasoning presented itself to Locke once more — maybe it would help some.

He let his eyes rest upon Bert's features, seeking some sort of answer, some assurance to the doubts that clouded his mind.

Bert caught his glance, grinned. "We got a deal?"

Locke hesitated a moment. He nodded briefly.

Beahm had satisfied himself as to the dead outlaws. His attention now shifted to the saddlebags lying between them and the fire.

"That the stage money?"

He knelt down beside the leather pouches, keeping his gun trained on Locke and Whitcomb. He released the buckles, pulled free the straps and thrust his hand into the inside. A look of pleasure crossed his broad face when his fingers touched the packets of currency.

"It all here?"

"Every dollar," Bert said.

"Fine, fine," Beahm murmured contentedly. He replaced the straps, pulled them tight in the buckles. He straightened up, leaving the saddlebags where they lay. A serious frown on his features, he glanced at the two men.

"Tell you what I've got a mind to do. No point in me riding all the way back to Three Forks. This job's all wound up now. I'll take the money and go on in to Denver. Can check it in at the office there. Locke, I'll put the prisoner in your custody. You turn him in to the marshal."

Locke listened to the investigator's words. He again had that strange feeling about Mathew Beahm, that he had experienced earlier that day, that possibly the man was not all he professed to be. And there was something wrong with the plan he had just outlined; it did not seem natural or at all logical.

He said, "Don't you have to get Carey and file a complaint or file charges or whatever it is?"

Beahm shrugged. "No point in it. All the bunch is dead but this one. And the marshal's got enough on him without any complaint from me. I've got the money.

That's the main thing I'm — the company is interested in."

Locke said. "Lot of it there. Too much for one man to be carrying alone. Wouldn't be near so risky if you'd take it back to Three Forks and ship it out on the stage or get yourself an escort."

"Got myself one," Beahm said then. "Two men been working for me. I'll just take them along."

Tilton and Morgan. They had slipped Locke's mind. But they did little to convince him that all was well. The thought crossed his mind that Beahm was no employee of the stage company at all, that he was a fake, an imposter. He was too anxious to get his hands on the money, too indifferent to punishing the men involved in the robbery. But surely Hazen Carey knew the man or had checked on him! There, he suddenly realized, was his own out if it did later develop that Beahm was nothing more than another outlaw. If the marshal accepted Beahm, then they could not blame Locke for believing, too.

But all things would go for naught if the money now fell into the hands of another thief. It could even tend to further complications and delays for himself. But if he and Bert brought Beahm in and the man was proven to be an outlaw, it could stand to help Bert a great deal! He slid a look at Whitcomb, moved his head up and down gently.

"When he picks up the saddlebags."

Bert nodded.

Beahm flung him a quick glance. "What was that? What did you say?"

Locke grunted. "Nothing. Just cussing my luck a bit."

Beahm continued to stare at him for a long moment, suddenly no longer the easy, affable man he had been. He stepped nearer to Bert Whitcomb's gun. With a side motion of his foot, he kicked it off into the brush.

He faced the two men. "Now, I'll be walking out of here to my horse," he said in low, clear words. "You won't be able to see me, once I'm beyond the firelight, but I'll be watching you. Every step of the way. Both of you stand where you are for five minutes — five minutes, you get that? Then you can do what you please."

Locke watched the man move back to where the saddlebags lay. He waited until Beahm had bent his knees, had crouched to pick up the leather pouches.

"Now!" he yelled and launched himself straight at the man.

They went down in a tangled, threshing heap. Locke was aware of Beahm lashing out, felt the power of the big man's great strength as a fist drove into his chest. Another smashed into his jaw. He had a fragmentary glimpse of Bert Whitcomb chopping downward at Beahm's face with the heel of his hand, delivering a murderous blow.

Beahm avoided it. At the instant of collision, Locke had grasped the hand in which the investigator held his pistol. He had carried it down with the weight of his body, pinned it to the dusty floor of the bowl. Now he saw that the man had worked it free, that he was striving to bring the weapon into the clear for a shot.

He clutched at the gun, only inches from his face. It blasted through their straining grunts, deafening him. The bright flash blinded him, powder stung his skin and smarted his eyes. He immediately caught the acrid smell of burning cloth — whose, he could not tell.

The bullet had gone wild. He struck out from his half-prone position, aiming for Beahm's jaw, but he was in an awkward way and he could get no leverage behind himself and therefore, no strength in the blow. It skidded off Beahm's chest, grazed his stubbled chin lightly. The investigator was endeavoring to get the pistol into use again. Locke lashed out at his arm, struck it but it did not dislodge the gun from his grasp.

He saw Bert Whitcomb then. He had the saddlebags containing the money, was crawling swiftly for the wall of blackness beyond the fire's dying glow. He tried to shout, to stop him with words but Whitcomb had one thing in mind; escape with the money while Locke and Beahm fought it out. That truth drove into John Locke and filled him with a wild, flaming anger.

This had been Bert's intention all the way!

Seething with rage he struck out at Beahm, venting his feelings on that man. Beahm grunted, rolled to one side. He caught sight of Bert at that moment, just starting to rise to his feet and run. Beahm wrenched free of Locke. He fired quickly, off hand. Locke saw Bert jolt from the solid impact of the heavy bullet, go forward to his knees. In the next instant Beahm was whirling upon him, using the gun as a club. The man's face was distorted with hate, streaked from sweat and dust.

"You think you two'll get away with my money —" he screamed and lashed out with his weapon.

Locke dodged the vicious blow. He rolled

hard at the investigator, onto his arm, again pinned him down. He smashed a hard right fist, heavy with the desperation of the moment, into Beahm's jaw. Beahm's eyes fluttered. He struggled wildly to pull himself loose.

Locke drove another iron hand into the man's unprotected jaw, the blow having its double reaction in that Beahm's head in turn rapped sharply against the unyielding ground. Locke lifted his balled hand once more, brought it down with all the strength he could muster.

"For calling me a ridgerunner —" he gasped.

Beahm groaned and went limp beneath him. Locke lay still for a moment, sucking for breath, and watched the big man closely. He was out cold, he was not shamming. He rolled away, got to his feet. He picked up Beahm's pistol, tearing it from the man's nerveless fingers, jammed it into his own holster. He wheeled to Bert. He had been hit hard. He took a full step, halted.

Bert Whitcomb was gone.

He was not lying at the edge of the firelight where he had fallen. Locke hurried forward. Perhaps he had dragged himself off into the darkness where he could lie unseen. In that next moment John Locke knew he was wrong. The quick drum of a running horse told him Bert had escaped. He had managed to reach his mount, get into the saddle and, with the saddlebags of money, flee to the east.

A bitter curse ripped from John Locke's lips. He swung about, cast a glance at Mathew Beahm. He was still unconscious, lying flat on his back, arms outflung. Locke wasted no more time. He returned, grabbed up his hat and started for the bay at a run. He found him first off, swung to the saddle. He wheeled him about and headed off into the heart of the brakes country, a grim determination to find and capture Bert Whitcomb filling him.

The night was still dark from its thick cloud cover. A distant flash of lightning and subsequent rumble of thunder announced, finally, the approach of the storm. He raised himself in his stirrups, turned his head to listen. The pound of Bert's horse was faint and rapid, a considerable space to the east. Whitcomb was moving fast, taking great chances over the broken, treacherous ground.

Locke was leaving it up to the bay. He was calling for speed but allowed the gelding to choose his own route so long as it was in the wake of Whitcomb. The going was hard;

loose sand and small gravel covered the floor of the wash up which they raced. Huge boulders lay scattered everywhere, forcing the horse to swerve and dodge and cut back and forth. Thick growths of Russian olive, brier, tamarack and mesquite choked the country and at times it was a matter of simply bulling their way through the tangled undergrowth that clung tenaciously to cloth and leather and horseflesh alike.

The bay tired quickly and Locke eased him down to a walk. He could no longer hear Whitcomb up ahead and wondered if he had stopped for a rest or, possibly because of his wound, had fallen from his horse. Or he could be beyond the range of sound. He couldn't see how Bert's horse could keep up the pace he had set for very long; no animal had that sort of stamina, however willing. And with Bert badly injured, as Locke knew he must be, and little help in the saddle, it would be much more difficult for him than the bay.

The first drops of rain fell soon after that. It was cool and refreshing and both Locke and the bay were the better for the shower — if a shower was all it would amount to. A continuing rain, if only for a few minutes could turn the arroyos and washes into roily torrents and complicate everything.

They topped a small ridge which angled across the brakes and there halted. It was completely dark and nothing beyond a fifty foot range was definitely discernible but John Locke spent several minutes studying the ground. He was remembering how he had overrun Bert and the two outlaws in the darkness earlier that night; he was worrying now that he might do so again. Only this time there would be no brightly glowing fire to catch his attention and bring him back. Bert, if still conscious, would take advantage of the blackness, make neither sound nor light.

The rain ceased. Locke strained his eyes seeking to pierce the solid invisibility that surrounded him. In that next moment a broad flash of lightning lit up the world about him with startling clarity. He had a glimpse, a very brief one, of a horse and rider several hundred yards ahead ascending a short slope. It was over before he could note any details, only that it was a man on horseback. It had to be Bert Whitcomb, he decided. No one else would be abroad in the desolate brakes on such a wild night.

He put the bay into motion, once again feeling the steady drumming of raindrops on his back as the storm commenced anew.

He rode slowly on, able to keep the slope up which he had last seen Bert fixed in his mind by the sporadic flares of light. Wet to the skin, he was beginning to feel the chill and the occasional gusts of cold wind which struck at him and cut to the bone.

Again the bay was having trouble. Water had begun to stand, to run in ankle-deep currents along the floor of the wash. Feeder arroyos already were spilling their accumulated loads of silted water into the broad flats of the brakes. Soon it would be dangerous to remain on low ground. Locke looked anxiously ahead, waited for the next blanket of light. He should be close to the hill up which he had seen Whitcomb riding.

Topping it would put him on high ground. It would be wise to reach that crest and there wait until the storm was over. Bert, if he were able to think, would realize the necessity and do likewise in some similar place. His horse, assuming Bert was in no condition to consciously do anything, would halt of his own accord. Animals, native to the country, quite often showed far more intelligence in such matters than their masters.

The flash came. He found he was at the foot of the slope, just starting the climb. It was not a hill but well above the floor of the wash and therefore beyond the reach of the water which was turning the brakes into a wide, flowing riverbed. There appeared to be timber or growth of some sort on the crest of the rise. This made Locke feel better. He should be able to find shelter of sorts for himself and the gelding from the driving rain.

They reached the top. The bay came to a sudden, jarring halt. Locke peered ahead through the intense blackness. Lightning flashed, to the north now as the storm swept on. A horse stood in the trail, a rider doubled over the saddle. Bert Whitcomb, without doubt. Locke came off the bay quickly but warily, uncertain now of the man he once had considered his closest friend. He drew his gun, approached cautiously. It was Whitcomb, all right, but the caution was unnecessary. Bert was not conscious.

Locke gathered the reins of the horse and those of his own bay and waited for the next explosion of light. It broke the solid wall of night a moment later, flickering bluely for a short time but long enough to reveal to Locke his position. A thin stand of brush lay to his right, just over the brow of the hill. He led the horses into it at once. It did not offer complete shelter from the rain and wind but it helped considerably and he was grateful for it.

He lifted Bert from the saddle, laid him out on the soaked ground. There was little he could do for the wounded man other than bind up the ugly, puckered hole Beahm's bullet had made which was in almost the identical position of the one that had caused Starr Whitcomb's death. For him, as it had been with his older brother, it was only a matter of time; a few hours at most.

A fire, of course, was out of the question. He had no dry matches and there was no wood capable of being burned. Even had it been possible to overcome those two problems, he still would have been reluctant to start any blaze for it would serve as a beacon to immediately draw Mathew Beahm down upon them.

He made Whitcomb as comfortable as possible. The rain began to slacken, dwindled to a thin patter. Locke, feeling the drag of the hours at him, placed his back against a thick clump of brush, dozed fitfully. He awakened once when Bert groaned loudly and muttered something feverishly; again when one of the horses stepped upon a dead branch, broke it. He was intensely cold, soaked through and when he opened his eyes for a final time that night, near daylight, it was a comforting thought to know the sun would soon be out, bringing warmness.

He rose, stamped his feet vigorously to start blood circulating through his congealed system. He glanced at Whitcomb. The man still slept. His color was unnaturally bright but he breathed fairly regularly. There was a pinched look to his mouth, though, and his lidded eyes appeared to have sunk deep into his skull. Locke stood for a time considering him and then turned away to where the horses grazed on the scanty grass of the hill.

When he returned a few minutes later the wounded man was awake. He knelt down beside him, his face still, unsure of his own emotions. Bert Whitcomb had failed him at every turn. Now, with death not far off in the background, he was at a loss as to how he should feel.

Bert managed a faint smile. "Reckon I fixed things up good this time, Johnny."

Locke nodded, made no comment.

"No need to tell me how bad it is. I know. I got a hunch this is it. What happens now?"

Locke shrugged. "Maybe if you could ride, I could get you to a doctor —"

"Not much use in that. What about that

fellow, Beahm?"

Locke waved his hand toward the west. "Out there somewhere. Hunting us, most likely. Him and his two men. I expect those shots last night drew them in."

"Might as well turn the money over to him."

Locke shook his head. "No, not to him. He's no stage company man, I'm dead certain of it now. I figure he's just another outlaw trying to get his hands on it. I don't know how he fooled Hazen Carey and the others but he has, sure enough."

Whitcomb stirred. "What do you figure to do then?"

"Get the money to Carey. Then I'll know it will end up at the right place."

Whitcomb hesitated a moment. He looked straight at Locke. "Johnny, I'd like to turn that money in to Carey myself. Like you've been wanting me to do."

Locke returned his gaze, his expression not changing, revealing nothing.

Locke moved his shoulders slightly. "Long ride and probably be a hard one if Beahm and his crew gets on our tail. Doubt if you could stand it."

"I can stand it," Whitcomb said grimly. "I'll stay alive long enough to reach Carey. After that it won't matter. Never asked many favors of you, Johnny, but I'm asking this one now. Let me do this."

Locke said, "All right with me, but I'll have to tie you in the saddle. And once we start there'll be no stopping for anything if Beahm spots us."

"Just tie me tight," Whitcomb said. "I want to get there. Seems real important to me now."

Locke arose and walked to where the horses still grazed. He led them back to where Whitcomb lay, anchored them. He lifted the wounded man to his saddle and with his own rope, secured him against falling. Bert groaned once or twice during the operation and when Locke glanced up to him after he had finished, his face was drained white.

"You sure this is what you want?" Locke asked.

Bert said, "The only thing. Let's get started."

Locke fastened a short lead rope to Bert's sorrel horse and swung to the saddle. He sat for a moment considering the best route to follow on the return trip across the brakes. Undecided, he rode to the crest of the hill, threw his glance over the trail he had covered those previous hours. It could be the fastest and easiest route would be to

— His thoughts came to an abrupt stop.

Mathew Beahm was just below, not over a quarter of a mile away.

12

He wheeled back from the ridge at once, hopeful that Beahm had not seen him. But it made little difference, he realized in that next moment. The rain which had been a boon in that it washed away the tracks their horses had made before, now was an enemy; it permitted the ground to record plainly their every movement.

He glanced at Bert. The man was again in a state of semiconsciousness, only vaguely aware of his actions. He turned his attention to the east. The land, rough and wild, lay before them. It offered ample cover from Beahm's searching eyes but it led to nowhere — and in the opposite direction to Three Forks.

To the north the rugged boundary of the brakes was a line of unbroken cliffs, not high but impossible for a horse to climb. South, lay the broad expanse of the brakes at its worst, eventually terminated by similar formations of bluffs. He studied the area with half shut, thoughtful eyes. If he could delay long enough, until just the proper moment when Mathew Beahm would be on the slope approaching the crest where he and Bert Whitcomb now waited, an escape might be accomplished. They could ride off the hill, circle it near its base and come back onto the trail on its western side. In so doing they would place themselves on the route that would lead them to Three Forks; but it would also place them in a precarious position. Their lead on Beahm would have been narrowed dangerously.

He considered the advisability of simply waiting for Beahm, of making a stand. He now had a weapon, the pistol he had wrenched from the investigator's fingers after the fight in the hollow. But he dismissed that thought. Tilton and Morgan would now be somewhere nearby. Gunshots would bring them in a hurry and, hampered by the helpless Bert, he would be waging a hopeless battle.

Coming to a decision, he dismounted and moved quickly back to the crest once again. Beahm had reached the base of the incline. There was no more time to lose. He returned to the bay quickly. Mounting up, he took the lead rope to Bert's horse in his hand and rode off the trail, heading deliberately into the thicker brush off to his right. He wished there was some way he could remove the tracks of the horses, showing plainly behind them. If it had been dry and dusty it would have been simple enough to brush them away with a leafy branch from one of the shrubs. But on the soft, muddy surface of the ground they were now deeply imprinted and there was nothing he could do about it.

The gradual descent along the pathless slope of the hill was slow and tricky. The horses continually slipped and several times Locke thought they would fall. But they managed, somehow, to keep their footing. Bert groaned in a low, painful way at every sudden move his sorrel made but the ropes held him firmly to the saddle and Locke spent no time worrying about that.

They reached the foot of the hill and stopped. Locke threw a glance to the rim, now a hundred yards or so above them. He hoped to see some sign of Beahm, proof that he had gained the summit. Thick brush and a huge pile of rock blocked his view and he could not tell. He would simply have to gamble on it. If it was as he expected, Beahm was at that very moment studying the tracks where they had spent the last few hours of the previous night. If, for some reason he had halted, had not continued on upward but yet remained on the slope, it would be a different problem. Beahm would spot them immediately when they rejoined the trail. There would be no choice then except to fight.

He checked the ropes that bound Bert Whitcomb to his horse, found them secure, and pushed on. It was somewhat easier now, despite the lack of a definite path, as the horses were moving on a level plane. They skirted the hill, reached a point where the main path was plainly visible. Locke halted and, leaving Bert and the horses behind, proceeded on foot. He climbed up onto a low knoll which afforded an unobstructed view of the slope. It was barren. Beahm was on the opposite side, puzzling over the numerous prints in the mud. It was working as Locke had planned. By the time the man figured out where the tracks led, they should be well on their way.

He hurried back to the bay, swung onto the saddle. With the lead rope to Bert's horse looped about his hand, he started forward at a fast walk. They completed the circling of the hill, reached the trail. He threw a glance at the crest behind them. Beahm was not to be seen. He was still on the far side. He urged the bay into a slow lope, having trouble with Whitcomb's sorrel which didn't follow well. But after a few yards the horse got the idea and they began to gain ground across the floor of the wash.

Where were Tilton and Morgan?

The bothersome question of that pair's whereabouts again presented itself to John Locke. They should have been somewhere near Beahm yet he had seen no signs of them. Were they out in the broken and brushy depths of the brakes, just waiting for him to turn up? Had Beahm stationed them at some strategic point along the trail, anticipating just such a move as he had made?

He began to watch ahead more carefully, sacrificing some degree of speed for safety. Several times, when he reached a slightly higher elevation above the tortuous route, he glanced over his shoulder, searching for Beahm. He never once caught sight of the man. And, at such times, he would also study the country ahead, watching sharp for the smallest movement, the faintest bit of color that might mark the presence and location of Tilton or Morgan. They, too, were not to be seen.

But they were there. He knew it. Mathew Beahm would not attempt to work through so wild and rugged a country as the brakes without their help. Locke was certain they had put in their appearance soon after the fight in the hollow that night before. Locke would have had them out as flankers; he would be using them for that same purpose again.

The sun broke over the eastern horizon, immediately warm and comforting. The chill faded slowly from Locke's tall frame and his muscles, stiff and cramped, began to loosen up. He glanced at Bert Whitcomb. He appeared to be unaware of the warming air, of anything at all. He rode slumped forward in the saddle, like a sack of grain, rocking with the motion of the horse. His features were strained, his eyes closed as if a great weariness weighted them down. But he was alive. As Locke watched he opened his mouth and licked at his dry lips.

Locke found Red Tilton a few minutes after that.

They had paused on the crest of a long running ridge which laced across the entire breadth of the brakes. Tilton, unexpectedly, was standing in full view a short quarter mile distant. It was at a point close to the mouth of the huge wash. Locke swung his attention to the opposite side. Morgan was stationed there.

He realized then what Beahm had done. He had left the pair to stand guard at the entrance, or exit, of the brakes, and had gone on ahead alone to search through the rocks and brush. If he overrode his quarry and flushed them out, they would immediately be trapped in between the three men.

John Locke pulled below the horizon and considered. He had no choice except to go on. Three Forks lay beyond the brakes. Not far, ten or twelve miles at the most on a good road. Still, he could not afford gunplay with Tilton. Such would bring both Beahm and Morgan down upon them in quick order. And Beahm, likely, was not far behind now. Although he had seen nothing of the big man since early that morning, he knew he was somewhere along the trail, patiently dogging their tracks. Whatever he did would have to be done quietly; he must bluff their way through, somehow.

He put the bay in motion and with Whitcomb and the sorrel close at his rear, he rode straight for the redheaded cowboy. He took a moment to remove his pistol, tuck it inside his shirt to give the impression of being unarmed. This, he felt, would allay Tilton's first suspicions.

One thing proved to be in his favor. When

he drew near the man he saw that Morgan, at the opposite side of the wash, was no longer visible. A tall stand of tamarack cut him from view. That made it some easier. Tilton heard them coming before he saw them. He was standing in front of his horse, gun drawn, watching intently when Locke and Whitcomb emerged from the brush. Locke did not wait to be challenged.

"Hey, Red! We're coming in!"

Tilton, uncertain, remained silent. He watched them ride up through narrowed eyes. Locke felt the pressure of the moments crowding down upon him like a tremendous weight. If Beahm should be nearer than he thought, should suddenly rush from the wash and sing out an alarm, it would all be over. Mentally he calculated his chances for reaching inside his shirt, grabbing the gun he had hidden there and using it in case just such an event occurred. The odds would be terrible.

"Where's Matt?" Tilton's face was an expressionless mask. Locke saw his eyes touch the empty holster at his side.

Locke drew to a halt near him. "Swung over to get Morgan. Be here in a minute."

The redhead lifted his glance to Whitcomb. "That the jasper that walked off with the money?"

Locke said, "That's him. About gone. Matt put a bullet in him."

"How come you bringin' him in?"

"Like I been trying to tell everybody, I'm not mixed up in this thing. Just happened along."

"What you doin' here now?"

"Still trying to get out of the country. Run into Beahm and Whitcomb last night. Sort of got caught between them I guess you might say."

Tilton relaxed a notch. "What about the money, Matt find it?"

"He did. There in those saddlebags on Whitcomb's sorrel."

Tilton moved up next to Bert. He holstered his pistol, reached for the straps and buckles of the leather pouches. In that moment John Locke acted. He drew his gun — Beahm's — swiftly, brought it down in a blurred arc. It struck Tilton across the top of his head. He dropped without a sound.

Locke touched the bay with his spurs and they moved quickly out, dragging the reluctant sorrel behind them as they climbed out of the brakes, up onto the open prairie. He glanced back. Tilton still lay where he had fallen. There was no sign of Beahm and Morgan still waited at the far side of the wash.

He yanked impatiently at the sorrel's lead rope, trying to straighten out the stubborn horse. They had no time to lose. The bay broke into a lope and the sorrel, at last, settled down to follow. They crossed the open ground, passed through the first out-thrusting patch of timber and then were on the main road to Three Forks.

Locke drew a deep breath. It would be easier now. He dropped back, looped the sorrel's lead rope over Bert's saddle horn. It would be simpler to drive the horse ahead of him now than to continue to lead. And it should be considerably faster.

He eased farther back, until he was beside Bert. The wounded man rode with his eyes closed tight. Now he opened them, looked tiredly about and finally placed them on Locke.

"Much more to go?" he asked in a ragged voice.

"Not so far now," Locke assured him. "Worst is over."

Whitcomb grinned. "Doubt if I can hold out much longer. Feels like I'm breakin' in two ever time this damned nag hits bottom."

"You'll make it," Locke said.

"Sure, sure. Got to make it. One thing I've got to do." He stopped, then, "Johnny?"

"Yeah?"

"Could be I won't be doing much talking after I get to Carey. Want you to know this. I'm sorry for all the hell I caused you. And everybody else. Wanted you to know that."

"Forget it," Locke said. "You might come through this yet. Main thing now is to get to town."

"Sure, kid, sure. Don't worry about it. I'll make it."

Locke said, "I'm going to get you up ahead. Then if Beahm and his boys are following, I'll hold them back. You'll be riding on alone. Understand?"

Bert nodded. "I still got that money, Johnny?"

"Right there in your saddlehags."

Bert Whitcomb said, "Good. I'll see that Carey gets it."

Locke slapped the sorrel on the rump, sent him forging ahead. The horse would stay on the road; all that was needed now was to keep him running. Tired as he was, he likely would try to stop. Locke half turned in his saddle, threw a backward glance over the route they had just traveled. His heart quickened. Three riders were in sight, coming on fast. It did not take a second look to tell who they were: Matt Beahm, Morgan and the redhead, Tilton.

13

Locke turned to Whitcomb. His sorrel was already beginning to slow down. He spurred the bay up until he was once again along side. He leaned over, looked closely at Bert. The man's eyes were half open while pain distorted his features.

"Try to keep that horse running!" he shouted. "They're coming up behind us fast!"

Bert Whitcomb nodded vaguely. It was doubtful if he understood the meaning of all the words but he apparently did comprehend the need for speed on the part of his horse. He buckled forward in the saddle, grasped the reins and the sorrel began to increase his pace. Locke had a moment's wonder as to the advisability of cutting the ropes that bound Whitcomb to his horse, thus enabling him to ride better. But he knew that would be a mistake, even if there was time to do so. Weak as Bert was he could never stay on the sorrel.

He swiveled his attention to Beahm and his pair of riders. They were coming fast, riding hard. It would be a hopeless task, trying to outride them. Their horses were in far better condition than the bay and the sorrel. His only solution was to drop back, delay them in some way and allow Bert to reach town with time enough to surrender himself to Hazen Carey or someone else in authority.

The bay was blowing hard. Locke pulled him down to a trot. Ahead the sorrel was beginning to draw off but he could not hold such a pace for long. And it was still miles to Three Forks. He glanced at Beahm and the others. They were startlingly near but, too, their own horses were starting to weaken, the hard run from the brakes having taken its toll of their strength.

Locke watched them closely, content to allow the pursuit to continue in such a manner. Beahm, he guessed, was mulling things over in his mind, sizing up the situation. He would realize he must get by Locke to reach Bert Whitcomb and the money; that he must do it soon for Three Forks lay ahead and once Bert gained the outskirts of the town it would be too late.

Locke saw them bend lower over their

horses, saw the animals lengthen their strides and speed up. Locke did not press the bay. He allowed him to continue on at his trot. The gap between Beahm and his men and Locke began to close. Locke drew the pistol he had taken from Beahm, held it experimentally in his hand. It was a lighter model than his own heavy-framed .45 and it did not feel right. But there was nothing he could do about that. He glanced once more at the approaching riders. Almost within range now.

He touched the bay with his spurs, pushing him up to a slow, easy lope. It would be easier to shoot from that pace than at the trot. He raised himself in the stirrups, twisted half about. He took careful aim at the nearest man, pressed the trigger. The bullet went low, digging into the ground ahead of the riders. He was misjudging the weapon. Its lighter weight was throwing him off.

He drew back the hammer again. This time he made no allowances for the gun but held it on Morgan's breast as closely as he could. He fired. Morgan folded suddenly, swayed in the saddle wildly. His horse, off stride, angled off the road and began to slow down. Beahm and the redhead pulled in beside him.

But it was only momentarily. Gunshots broke out behind him and bullets began to whine overhead and thud into the roadway around him. His own gun must be near empty, he concluded. He bent low over the bay, called upon him for more speed. With his left hand he flipped open the loading gate of the pistol. He punched out a spent cartridge, sought to replace it with a fresh one from his belt. The bullet would not fit. He looked more closely at the gun. It was a different caliber than his; a .41 instead of a .45.

He swore softly at that bit of ill luck. The shooting behind him had ceased. Beahm and Tilton had been forced to reload, also, he assumed. He checked his weapon again, patiently removed the rest of the empty shell casings. Finished, he smiled grimly. He had one good cartridge left.

Bert Whitcomb was a hunched shape on his horse a few yards ahead. They could not be far from town. If Beahm and Tilton could be held off a few more minutes, they would never catch up to the sorrel. He looked back. The two men had abandoned their shooting, were again putting their efforts to overtaking the bay and the sorrel. They were coming up fast. Locke set the last bullet in the pistol into a firing position, replaced the weapon in his holster. It would be his final effort, if it came down to that.

The road slipped beneath the bay in a blur of grays and brown. Where the horse was getting his strength Locke could only wonder — and hope that he could continue. But he was bound to break soon. They reached the first, long bend in the road that marked the beginning of a series of switchbacks leading into the town. They were nearer than he had thought; being away five years, he guessed he had forgotten exactly how the land lay.

He ventured another glance to the rear, wondering if Beahm would now give it up, abandon his determination to get the money; or would he press on, keep at it until the very edge of Three Forks was before them. He could still accomplish his purpose, Locke knew. If they could remove him, then bring down the sorrel with a well placed bullet, the saddlebags with its packets of money would be in their hands.

It was what they had in mind. Locke saw it in the next moment. Beahm had pulled a rifle from his saddle boot, was watching for a chance to use it. The second of the sharp, double curves in the route was upon them. Here, the formation of the land changed. The road had left the plains, now worked its way through a lengthy row of buttes that crowded in close on either side, forming a sort of narrow canyon.

It was perfect country for the bushwhacker and that thought gave John Locke an idea. Here would be an ideal place to make a stand. If he was to halt Beahm and his redheaded companion, Tilton, here was the spot and now was the time. Even if he failed, the delay created would allow sufficient time for Bert Whitcomb to reach the settlement and complete his purpose.

He slowed the heaving bay, angled him off toward the right hand side of the road. Halting, he leaped from the saddle. Drawing his pistol, he trotted to the opposite side and waited. Beahm and Tilton would first catch sight of the bay, standing with empty saddle. They would wonder, would immediately slow down, suspecting a trick. Then he would make his play. He grinned sardonically. *Make his play!* One bullet against two desperate, determined gunmen! The odds were a little lopsided.

"Got you covered, Locke! Don't move!"

The shouted command reached down to him from the crown of the bluff under which he stood. Luke Ford! Of all the men he wanted less to see at that moment, it was the pigheaded deputy.

"Saw you ridin' hell bent down the road! Figured I'd catch up with you right about here. You ain't givin' me the slip this time. Throw down that gun!"

Locke, hands away from his sides, half lifted, watched the curve ahead around which Beahm and Tilton would shortly appear, shook his head.

"Not now. Got business with a couple of your old friends."

"Old friends?" Ford echoed. "What kind o' talk is that?"

"Just what it sounds like."

Ford was having none of it. He said, "You goin' to throw down that gun? Better be quick about it!"

Where were Beahm and Tilton? They should have reached the curve by then, should be coming around it. In the breathless, still hush of the morning, his voice seemed overloud as he replied to the deputy, sought to keep him out of the way until the matter with Beahm and his redheaded companion was satisfied.

"Not now, Luke. Wait until I've finished. Then I'll go along with you if I'm still alive. If you're so anxious to use that pistol of yours, come on down here and side me. I'm facing up to two men."

"Two men — who?"

"Beahm and Tilton."

"The stage line investigator —"

"He's no investigator!" Locke cut in. "He's just another outlaw after that stolen money. Same with Tilton and Morgan, only Morgan's out of it now. I put a bullet into him back down the way."

Ford muttered something under his breath, then said, "Sounds like some more of your tricks. You ain't catchin' me again!"

"No trick," Locke replied, his gaze fastened to the bend in the road.

"That money. You got it on you?"

Locke shook his head. "Bert Whitcomb's got it. He went on ahead to turn it in to the marshal."

"Now I know it's some sort of trick!" Ford exclaimed triumphantly. "Bert Whitcomb wouldn't be doin' no such thing as that! Not Bert! Now, you throw down that gun! Hear me?"

John Locke stiffened. It was too late for any further talk. Matt Beahm, closely followed by Tilton, suddenly appeared in the road. Behind him he heard an ominous click as Luke Ford cocked his weapon.

"You goin' to drop your gun?" the deputy demanded.

Chills clawed at John Locke's spine. He could not turn to face the man, could only keep his gaze ahead on Beahm and Tilton. But where did the greatest danger lie? Ford, shamed and disgraced personally, so he thought, by Locke's two successful escapes from him, would take no chances on it happening again. He would see only vindication in bringing in Locke — dead or alive. It would not matter which.

"Locke — how about it?"

Beahm and Tilton were approaching slowly, allowing their horses to walk. They had seen the bay, suspected something, and now came on warily.

"You goin' to do what I say?" Luke Ford demanded in a threatening voice. "You goin' to drop that gun?"

Locke rode out the terrible moments. The crash of the deputy's gun, the shock of a bullet into his back would be no great surprise. He steeled his nerves, made no sign of having heard the man. He watched Beahm and Tilton narrowly, waited until they reached that point in the road he had mentally marked as a deadline.

"Far enough!"

He barked out his warning and moved away from the bluff to the center of the road.

Tilton hauled in sharply. Beahm slowly continued on. He had given the redhead the rifle and he now carried his hands close to his hips while a hard grin creased his broad face.

Locke's hand dropped nearer his gun. "Hold it there!"

Beahm shook his head, pressed on. "No time to waste on you, drifter. I'm going on by."

"No," Locke answered in a dust dry voice. "You'll never make it.'

"I'll make it," Beahm insisted quietly. "You try to stop me and Red will take care of you."

"Odds have changed, friend," Locke replied. "Look up above me. That's the deputy. He'll look after Red. It's just you and me."

It was pure bluff. He was not even certain that Ford was still on the hill behind him or that he would help, if he were. But it shook Beahm's confidence. Locke saw him glance upward quickly, saw a frown cloud his face. Over beyond him Red Tilton stirred uneasily in his saddle.

"Now, I ain't —" Ford's protesting voice began but Beahm cut him short.

"You ain't stopping me!" he shouted. "I was two months finding a deal like this and no saddlebum is going to knock me out of it!"

He slashed his horse with his spurs. Locke saw him swing his gun around, level it for a quick, close shot. He spun away, drew as he did. *One bullet!* That warning flashed through his mind. *One bullet!* It had to go true or he was a dead man.

He brought the unfamiliar weapon up in a fast arc. It lined with Beahm's twisting shape. He held steady for the briefest fragment of time, fired. Beahm rocked to one side in the saddle. He straightened up, stared hard at Locke and fell heavily to the ground.

Locke pivoted to face Tilton. The redhead was still in the saddle. He met Locke's thrusting gaze, looked away.

"How about it, Red?" Locke called softly.

Tilton shook his head. "Not for me," he murmured.

A long sigh escaped Locke's lips. He kept the useless pistol leveled at the redheaded cowboy. "Drop that rifle then and come on over here. The marshal will want to talk to you."

Tilton complied, saying no more. When he was disarmed and waiting, Locke turned to Luke Ford.

"All right, deputy, come on down. I'm your prisoner. You can take me in — with Tilton, here."

"Take you in?" Ford repeated in a wary tone. "Sounds to me like another trick —"

Locke shook his head wearily. "No trick, Luke. Come on, let's go."

14

They rode into Three Forks a short time later, Locke, Tilton and Deputy Luke Ford. Several people were on the street and they gathered quickly about the three men when they halted before the marshal's office.

"Get down," Locke said to the redhead.

"Now, wait a minute there!" Ford began angrily. "I'm the deputy here. *You* get down, too, mister!"

Locke dismounted. Keeping Tilton before him, within easy reach, he started for the doorway of the jail. He glanced down the street. A man was leading Bert Whitcomb's sorrel toward the stable. The horse was fagged, almost near collapse. But Bert had made it. Seeing the sorrel there proved that.

"Come on, come on," Ford said impatiently. "Get on inside."

They crossed the narrow board walk and entered the building. Hazen Carey, Dean and several other men stood behind the marshal's desk. Whitcomb's saddlebags, with the packets of stolen money stacked beside them, lay on its scarred surface.

"Here's my prisoner, marshal," Ford said without any preliminaries. "Didn't get away from me this time!"

Hazen Carey stared at the deputy with a steady, unrelenting gaze.

Locke asked, "How's Bert?"

Without moving his head the lawman said, "Dead."

John Locke lowered his eyes for a moment. Then, "Did he make it in time to talk?"

Fred Dean spoke up. "We got the whole story, Johnny. All of it."

"Well, here's some more to it!" Luke Ford broke in. "Maybe you only know half of it! Locke, here, just killed that feller, Beahm. Said he potted Morgan, too, but I don't know for certain about that. I brought Tilton along, too, so's there'd be a witness. It was a fair fight but Beahm bein' that stage company's investigator —"

"He was no investigator for the stage lines," Locke stated. "A little talk with Tilton ought to convince you of that."

Carey said, "I already know it. Got to thinking about it last night and checked with the Dangerfield people. Got an answer

174

to my telegram this morning. Beahm did work for them once, but not for over a year now."

Hazen Carey paused, noticed Locke's inquiring glance. "He fooled other lawmen, too. Still carried his old identification papers. Passed himself off as working for the Dangerfield line real easy."

Luke Ford said, "You tellin' me he wasn't no special investigator at all?"

The marshal shook his head. "Had himself a pretty smart thing going. When he'd hear of a coach holdup, he'd ride in, pass himself off as working for the stage company. When the money was recovered, he'd just take charge of it, saying he would personally take it in to the company's office. Only he'd keep it for himself. Guess it worked out right good, too, for him. They say he was a smart detective and usually was able to run down the outlaws that had robbed the stage."

Luke Ford was staring at Locke. "Then we don't want this jasper —"

"We should have listened to him at the start," Carey said, ruefully. "At least to what he said about himself. Only thing he was wrong about was the Whitcombs."

Locke shrugged. He had been wrong there; no use denying it. But Bert had made it up to some extent. He said, "Guess time can change people, marshal. Just didn't figure it would change Bert and Starr that much." He stopped, faced the old lawman. "Now, if you're through with me, I'll see about getting myself another horse and moving on. Could be I've lost that job that was waiting for me, already."

Fred Dean smiled. "No need for it now."

Locke switched his attention to the merchant. "No?"

"Before Bert died he signed a paper turning the Whitcomb place over to you. Said he wanted you to have it and figured Starr would like it that way, too. Not much point in your riding on to Wyoming for a foreman's job when you got a ranch of your own to look after here."

John Locke stared at Dean in disbelief. And then at Hazen Carey.

The lawman said, "He's right, son. It's all yours. Be a lot of hard work fixing it up, but the land is there. And so's the buildings. I reckon you won't have any trouble getting some stock together for a starter herd, either. People around here will be happy to lend you a hand. And there's all that reward money. The stage company will be paying off for Beahm. Thousand dollars, I think it is. And there'll be more for bringing in Bert Whitcomb and the money he had stolen."

"Forget that part of it," Locke said at once. "Bert turned himself in."

He tried to think of something else to say, to find words that would express his appreciation. They wouldn't come. He could only stand in the center of the hot, stuffy little room and mull over the wonder of it all.

Fred Dean said, "Someone else is waiting to help too, Johnny."

Locke glanced at the man, saw he was looking off beyond him, toward the doorway. He turned around slowly. Sally was just outside. The love shining through her eyes gave him the answer to all the questions that had haunted him.

He swung back to the men. "Thanks, marshal — all of you. Now, I guess I'd better go write a letter to the Walking W outfit in Wyoming. Want to tell them not to hold that job open for me. Won't be leaving here."

He nodded briefly to them and walked to where Sally waited. Taking her by the hand, he moved off down the street.

ABOUT THE AUTHOR

Ray Hogan is an author who has inspired a loyal following over the years since he published his first Western novel *Ex-marshal* in 1956. Hogan was born in Willow Springs, Missouri, where his father was town marshal. At five the Hogan family moved to Albuquerque where Ray Hogan still lives in the foothills of the Sandia and Manzano mountains. His father was on the Albuquerque police force and, in later years, owned the Overland Hotel. It was while listening to his father and other old-timers tell tales from the past that Ray was inspired to recast these tales in fiction. From the beginning he did exhaustive research into the history and the people of the Old West and the walls of his study are lined with various firearms, spurs, pictures, books, and memorabilia, about all of which he can talk in dramatic detail. Among his most popular works are the series of books about Shawn Starbuck, a searcher in a quest for a lost brother, who has a clear sense of right and wrong and who is willing to stand up and be counted when it is a question of fairness or justice. His other major series is about lawman John Rye whose reputation has earned him the sobriquet The Doomsday Marshal. "I've attempted to capture the courage and bravery of those men and women that lived out West and the dangers and problems they had to overcome," Hogan once remarked. If his lawmen protagonists seem sometimes larger than life, it is because they are men of integrity, heroes who through grit of character and common sense are able to overcome the obstacles they encounter despite often overwhelming odds. This same grit of character can also be found in Hogan's heroines and, in *The Vengeance of Fortuna West,* Hogan wrote a gripping and totally believable account of a woman who takes up the badge and tracks the men who killed her lawman husband by ambush. No less intriguing in her way is Nellie Dupray, convicted of rustling in *The Glory Trail.* Above all, what is most impressive about Hogan's Western novels is the consistent quality with which each is crafted, the compelling depth of his characters, and his ability to juxtapose the complexities of human conflict into narratives always as intensely interesting as they are emotionally involving. His latest novel is *Soldier in Buckskin.*

We hope you have enjoyed this Large Print book. Other Thorndike, Wheeler, Kennebec, and Chivers Press Large Print books are available at your library or directly from the publishers.

For information about current and upcoming titles, please call or write, without obligation, to:

Publisher
Thorndike Press
295 Kennedy Memorial Drive
Waterville, ME 04901
Tel. (800) 223-1244

or visit our Web site at:

http://gale.cengage.com/thorndike

OR

Chivers Large Print
published by BBC Audiobooks Ltd
St James House, The Square
Lower Bristol Road
Bath BA2 3SB
England
Tel. +44(0) 800 136919
email: bbcaudiobooks@bbc.co.uk
www.bbcaudiobooks.co.uk

All our Large Print titles are designed for easy reading, and all our books are made to last.